The Most
INTERESTING
Man in the World

J. L. ASHTON • JUSTINE RIVARD

Meryton Press

OYSTERVILLE, WA

Also by J. L. Ashton

A SEARING ACQUAINTANCE

MENDACITY AND MOURNING

THE MOST INTERESTING MAN IN THE WORLD

Copyright © 2019 by J. L. Ashton and Justine Rivard

ISBN: 978-1-68131-029-9

Cover design: Ellen Pickels and Janet Taylor
Cover image based on "Stamford Raffles" (1817) portrait by George Francis Joseph
Back cover images: stock.adobe.com
Layout: Ellen Pickels

Dedication

To our families, who have no idea what we are talking about and are smart enough not to ask questions.

The authors wish to own up to errant use of verbiage, Latin jokes, and the odd reference to magic carpets, etc. It's a comedy, after all.

Part I: Caveat Emptor

Buyer Beware

Netherfield Park was his at last!

The sun was high above and shining happily. The air was the precise temperature of heaven's breath. Grass grew under their feet, birds flew in the sky, and trees loomed over the fields. It was more promising, more exciting than Charles Bingley had remembered. *His* sky, *his* grass, *his* fields! He was a landed gentleman—or as good as. He pushed aside the slight sense of being overwhelmed by what lay ahead. After all, his friend Darcy would help with all those niggling details such as misplaced fence posts, faded wall coverings, and drainage issues, whatever those were. Surely, he could easily hire men to fix such minor annoyances. After all, Darcy might know everything there was to know about improperly placed fence posts, but it was madness to imagine him actually *touching* one. A gentleman would never do that, would he?

But oh, to have his own estate! To grow crops, tend fields, thatch roofs, and build dams! Not that he would be growing crops, thatching roofs, or building dams himself, of course. He had played at such things in his childhood, stacking pebbles and sticks in the stream behind his aunt's house and pulling up the occasional potato or turnip for her cook. "Such a good boy you are, wee Charles," dear Aunt Millie would coo before handing him a biscuit.

How he wished that she, with her kind smile and ready biscuit, had lived to see this day—this day of days! He, Charles Bingley, had his own estate.

For now. It was a lease—what Darcy called "an exercise in ownership." Darcy had long been master of his own grand estate, Pemberley, and owner of a house in town and estates in Ireland, Scotland, and (Bingley suspected) France, but no one spoke of properties in France these days. It simply was not done. There was a war on, after all.

He hoped, dearly hoped, that Darcy would be impressed with his acumen in choosing Netherfield Park for this exercise in ownership. His chest nearly burst with anticipation for the opinion of his most esteemed friend and adviser. No one knew more about managing a country estate than Darcy. He knew more than anyone did about everything: history, mathematics, geography, ancient languages, waistcoat selection, and proper comportment in gentlemen's clubs. It would take him but a moment to see the glory of Netherfield, or so Bingley hoped.

Now, at last, they were here. Bingley and Darcy reined in their horses at the top of a small rise from where they could see the house at Netherfield sparkling on this fine autumn day. Bingley gasped privately in silent joy and turned to Darcy with a jolly smile.

"Well, what do you think?" Bingley asked in breathless anticipation, gesticulating at the splendour before them and casting his glance towards the magnificent man and beast to his left. "Is it everything the agent said it would be? Shall I buy it straight away?" He had visited some weeks earlier to see the property before committing to renting it, and he had done it all by himself! Darcy had helped him select the place from a list of vacant properties the agent had provided, but Bingley was anxious to hear his friend's approval now that he actually set eyes on it.

"It is far too soon to say," Darcy replied before sighing heavily. "It requires time to get a true sense of things, does it not?"

A true sense of things? Bingley realised he had been asking himself a similar question about Darcy's state of mind only the week before. He had wondered whether something had happened over the summer months to make his usually reserved-but-ever-cordial friend turn so gloomy. At the time, he had thought it was just the weather. It had been a remarkably hot summer, and even now, in late September, the sun was still strong, especially after a long ride. Bingley always broke out in hives when the weather was too hot, especially under his cravat. Granted, he had never seen Darcy covered in hives—nor, truth be told, had he ever seen his friend *un*covered either, as Darcy was most fastidious—but one could never be too careful. For a moment, he scrutinised Darcy, searching for any sign of him scratching his neck or tugging at his neck cloth as Bingley so often did in the heat. But Darcy's hands remained steady near the stallion's mane, grasping the reins with a skilful, relaxed touch that he envied. He was glad to see his friend did not seem to be in need of the soothing creams or powders that Bingley favoured and, indeed, was currently wearing. His dear, departed mother had recommended a calendula cream that he found particularly effective. He would have to suggest it to Darcy next time he seemed in danger of developing hives.

Bingley returned his gaze to the house. "Nine chimneys, a ballroom, and a view of the tallest peak in Hertfordshire," he said whilst painstakingly pointing out each chimney, eagerly anticipating Darcy's response. After a prolonged moment of silence broken only by the shrill cries of birds that sounded unnervingly like Caroline, Bingley cleared his throat.

"Have you nothing to say of the place?"

"It is situated well on grassy land and appears to have windows in every room." Darcy shifted in his saddle. "And it is an easy distance from London."

"Yes!" Bingley cried, heartened by his friend's observations. He peered back at the road from which they had come and noticed a cloud of dust that could only indicate the carriage containing his sisters and Hurst was close to arriving at the house. So soon? That would not do at all.

"Shall we ride about for a bit to see whether the grounds are as astound-ingly beautiful as the house?" Bingley asked brightly. "Or are you too tired from the journey? Would you prefer to go to the house directly?"

Darcy glanced up and noted the imminent arrival of the carriage. "Yes, a quick ride would be just the thing." He spurred on his horse, and the two men trotted down the rise and away from the house as Bingley's sister Caroline poked her head out of the carriage window, waved her handkerchief, and called out, "Hallo!"

"Oh, look! A fine spot for a duck blind!" Bingley exclaimed, sneaking a quick peek over his shoulder at the carriage while pointing for Darcy's benefit in no particular direction. "There is nothing as thrilling as an excellent duck blind!"

"So it would be," Darcy said slowly, a hint of a smile creeping over his visage, "were there ducks and a pond on this side of the estate."

Bingley shrugged, less abashed at his error than he was happy to have amused his friend.

Presently, the horses topped a small hill, and Bingley pulled up, exclaiming in delight over the beauty that lay before them. It was a virtual rainbow of autumn wild flowers swaying gently in the breeze. Off in the distance, they could see cows idly grazing in a meadow, and the sky was blue and full of puffy clouds.

"I say, Darcy, have you ever seen such a lovely place? I never in my wildest dreams imagined that Hertfordshire would be so full of natural beauty."

"There is nothing especially remarkable about this place." Darcy sniffed. "It is all rather dull and completely indistinguishable from any other place in this part of the country."

"Certainly, it is nothing to Pemberley! Nothing could compare to Pemberley. Still, behold these wild flowers! The dramatic hills! Those exquisite cows over yonder! They are truly splendid." Bingley took a deep breath, quickly noting that he should avoid mentioning the less-than-exquisite bovine odour and forged ahead to a more interesting subject. "One can only imagine the beauty of the ladies in the area. Why, with such a background, how could they fail to be among the loveliest ladies in all of England?"

Darcy looked at him balefully. "Really, Bingley? Exquisite cows? This is not one of Constable's paintings. Doubtless the ladies here will be as uninteresting as the lacklustre landscape."

"Come now, Darcy, do not be such a starched fellow." Bingley laughed. "What has come over you lately? They may not hold a candle to the ladies in London, but surely the ladies here will be even more handsome than those we have seen on the way from town."

"Oh, you are certainly correct with your supposition." Darcy rolled his eyes. "How could I forget the beauty of the towns along the way—Biggleswade, Goat Bottom Howling, Scrooby, Scarthing Moor, Fearsome Wapping—and that such beauty was matched by the blushing countenances of the lovely lasses dwelling within?"

Bingley shook his head and lifted his hand to waggle a gloved finger. "You miss my point! Ladies outside of London boast a warm and natural prettiness." He saw Darcy's face remained full of doubt, perhaps even disgust. Bingley repressed the memory of a few angels—fair of face and full of grace—he had left behind in town. Or seen off to their family estates in the country. Thus, his point was proved. Ladies in the country were indeed as handsome as those in the city!

"You travelled frequently this past summer," Bingley added. "Did you not notice that the beauty of the landscape was reflected in the beauty of the ladies?"

"I fail to see how there could possibly be a connection."

"Do you not? I recall your commenting that Ramsgate was a hideous place and you had expected so much better from a town by the seaside. So I put it to you: Were the ladies there just as astoundingly ugly as the place itself? Did they have rough hands and weather-beaten faces from all the sea air?"

Ha ha! Bingley laughed to himself, imagining that the ladies in Ramsgate must look like sailors in the Royal Navy. Though what would that mean exactly? He was not sure. Maybe some wore eye patches and limped about on wooden legs. Oh, how tragic a sight that would be! No, wait…that was pirates, not sailors. Was there such a thing as a lady pirate? He thought perhaps there was, though he should not wish to meet one.

Darcy nodded his head in disgust. "You remember correctly, Bingley. Ramsgate was loathsome. I hope never to have the misfortune of setting foot there again as long as I live."

"Aha! So the ladies were that ill favoured, eh? You see, it is just as I suspected. Pray, go on! Are the ladies in Ramsgate afflicted with—?"

Darcy turned briefly from gazing at a stand of trees to look at Bingley. "As I said, my opinion of Ramsgate has nothing to do with the ladies there."

This struck Bingley as quite strange. His own opinions of a place *always* had to do with the ladies. For instance, he recently decided to take his leave of London and seek out an estate of his own upon discovering that not all the ladies in that city were wonderful. Well, one in particular was not: Miss Amelia Goodey. She was everything delightful at first. She adored canaries and large decorative ferns, and so did he! They got on well, he had thought, and all was good with Miss Goodey. Until it was not. He had to admit he began to tire of her after their third visit to the fern conservatory. The last straw, however, was when he noticed Darcy's apparent disapprobation of her. Something about her need to please her father and his banker? Or did he say baker? It had been a long evening after a long day, and Bingley was not sure what he had said, but Darcy clearly meant to warn him that she was a fortune hunter.

Bingley found that conclusion somewhat surprising since she was rumoured to have a dowry of thirty thousand pounds. Darcy was astute about these things though, having been the object of a plethora—or perhaps even two plethoras, so numerous were they—of eager ladies in the past; therefore, Bingley reckoned he had best take his friend's wise counsel. Miss Goodey's once-charming smile had somehow become overcrowded with teeth, and her once-lustrous locks looked more and more as if she were wearing a poodle on her head. An angel whose beauty was as faded as his affections made everything seem glum. London had simultaneously become dreary and unattractive. There *was* a connection between the beauty of a place and the beauty of its ladies, he was sure of it. If only he could convince Darcy he was right.

"I have not journeyed to the places you have. No tour of the Continent, no estate to inspect in Ireland or Scotland, no time in Bath or in Brighton." Bingley leaned forward and stroked Blackie's mane. Horses have such shiny hair! After a moment of admiration, he returned to his original course of thought. "Are not the ladies becoming in different ways in each place? Further north, you might find rosy cheeks and a preference for wool, while nearer the sea, perhaps bright eyes and a freshness of spirit?"

Darcy completed his perusal of the landscape and turned to Bingley. "Have you never visited London's galleries nor paused to gaze upon the portraits at Pemberley or Darcy House? A woman's looks, as a man's, owe less to the nature that grows around them than to the looks of their parents."

Bingley fell silent, pondering the points made by his older, wiser friend. Darcy was right, of course; he always was. For good or ill, children resembled their parents. He had his father's nose and eyes, just as Caroline did. He was well pleased by the resemblance. His sister was not though, and she devoted herself to using Gowland's lotion and ripe elderberries for a more ladylike appearance. Darcy had an exceptionally finely shaped nose; it was long and noble and placed perfectly above his mouth and centred between his eyes. Bingley had danced once with a girl whose eyes were set too close together, and he had felt scrutinised as if by a predator looking for its next meal. Shuddering, he forced himself back to his point. Darcy was being evasive on the subject of his visit to Ramsgate. He was overset with curiosity.

"Darcy, Ramsgate is a seaside town visited by families, and thus not all the ladies you saw there could have been called unpleasant reptiles. Mermaids, however…"

"Ramsgate has a multitude of deficiencies, but I would not rate the ladies among the worst."

Bingley seized on this statement eagerly. "Did a lady there catch your interest? Aha, one did! I knew it!"

He noted that Darcy's normally unreadable expression shifted slightly. Was that pain in his eyes? Regret? Yearning?

"No, Bingley," he replied wearily, looking off to stare with obvious disapproval at a half-dead oak tree. "It was not a trip for pleasure but for business. Ladies, be they reptiles or mermaids, were the least of my concerns."

Worry for Darcy mingled with eagerness to entertain him with the delights of Netherfield. Bingley would surprise his sisters and his friend with news of the assembly. A little music, a bit of dancing or sport, some good food and fellowship—that was the cure for any man's woes. Well, there *were* other things that could help, but Darcy would never go in for such activities, and certainly none of *those* were to be had in a small town such as Meryton. In any case, those things were best left to Darcy's outrageous cousin, the colonel, as they were more his province than Bingley's.

Noticing that the sun was getting lower in the sky, Bingley reckoned reluctantly that it was time to go to the house and face his sisters' wrath. Sometimes he secretly thought of them as the Gorgonzolas. Was that what they were called? He could never keep all those Greek myths straight: Theseus, Perseus, Hansel, Gretel; they all sounded the same. As for the Gorgonzolas, Caroline could sometimes seem like Methuselah herself, turning a man to stone with a single glance. No, no, not Methuselah. It was something like that though; he was sure. But he was so tired after the long ride; he would have to ask Darcy about it. Darcy always seemed to remember everything. He had the best memory of any man Bingley knew, and he had met quite a few men in his life.

"Shall we return to the stables? We cannot avoid the Gorgonzolas forever, you know."

"I beg your pardon?" Darcy turned nearly all the way around in his saddle to stare at him. Good Lord, how did he do that? He must be gripping his horse powerfully with those strong thighs of his. Darcy really had the best seat Bingley had ever set eyes on, maybe even better than the men in a picture book he had seen once—giant Mongol horsemen riding tiny little ponies, their feet nearly dragging on the ground while they sacked all of Byzantium. Or perhaps it was the Turks who had done that. History made for such dull reading. So many battles, marriages, and treaties signed by men with long names on unmemorable dates. And it was all so sad with the ghastly deaths, pillaging, looting, and crumbling temples. In any case, he wagered Darcy could turn and shoot a deer with a bow and arrow from a thousand paces at full speed without even falling off his horse. It was not easy, Bingley knew. He had suffered a dangerously skinned knee and a broken finger for his own efforts at it. But Darcy rode like a Centaur: smoothly, his dark tresses blowing handsomely back in the breeze, except when he wore a hat, as he did now.

Indeed Darcy's beaver sat perfectly atop his head. It had not been blown askew by the rush of wind as they rode, nor were there bits of leaves and road dust clinging to it. Bingley could not see his own hat, but a glance at his person showed him that Darcy's coat appeared less in need of a brushing than his own. He suspected that Darcy did not smell of sweat and horseflesh. Darcy once told him that a gentleman should not follow the example of Beau Brummell, but—perhaps due to his disdain of the Prince Regent—he did agree with the fashion arbiter that all gentlemen should smell of good washing and fresh clean air. It was a valuable bit of advice even though Bingley was fond of dusting powders and hair pomade.

According to Caroline, Darcy never smelt ill but exuded a heady mixture of fine leather and starch. She knew such things, or she at least spoke of such things as though she had some authority. As she had neither been courted nor spent much time with unmarried men, it was odd how much she knew from her observations. What was it she had said of Darcy? "If I could bottle his essence..." Bingley shuddered. Her words made him think of witchcraft. He had read of the witch trials both in England and America. Now *there* was history worth studying and remembering. How frightening it would be to repeat it.

Perhaps he should find that book and ensure Caroline read it as well. Perhaps Darcy had a copy and could lend it to him. Caroline would read it if it belonged to Darcy. Come to think on it, she might never return it.

"What was that about cheese, Bingley? I thought you were a Stilton man."

"Cheese?"

"You mentioned Gorgonzola, a cheese I tasted in Italy. We spoke of it after I returned from the Continent. As I recall, you said that if you were to eat blue cheese, it had better be 'good old English Stilton.'"

"Ah, cheese," Bingley drawled, startled and somewhat bemused by his learned friend mistaking mythical Greek harridans for Italian cheese. But hold! Could it be that those viragos were Roman? That might explain a few things. Darcy was always so particular about getting all the details correct. Glancing up, he saw that his friend was still staring at him, eyebrows raised in some small show of confusion. Or was it mirth? Oh, that would be splendid if he had cheered up his old friend even if it required humouring him about such a rare and silly mistake. Cheese it was!

"Yes, Stilton, as you say. I thought a bit of cheese and bread or a biscuit would sit nicely right now. All this riding does work up an appetite."

Some hours later, Bingley followed Darcy into the library for some port and manly conversation after the evening repast. His sisters were not pleased by the separation of the sexes. Caroline had gone on and on about their small party not needing to bow to town customs while Louisa sighed heavily and glared at her slumbering husband. How did the man fall asleep so regularly at the dining table, spoon in hand and serviette tucked into his collar? Bingley had once supposed Hurst's love of wine and whisky was the reason for his frequent lethargy, but of late, he wondered whether sleeping—or pretending to sleep—was the man's only escape from his wife and sister's company.

Bingley collapsed onto the settee while Darcy lounged against the mantelpiece. How could the man remain on his feet after such a day and such a meal? Bingley was utterly fatigued from the long ride in the hot sun, from listening to his sisters' bickering, and from eating an overwhelming amount of cheese both before and after the main meal.

Since he had assured Darcy he was so fond of Stilton, they had to have it for befores. Bingley had slipped quietly into the kitchen to ask Cook to add some to the cheese plate, and he put on a show of enjoying it. To be frank, he found it rather revolting. Who in their right mind would eat blue food?

Of course, his friend was correct, and he really did prefer uncomplicated, good old English cheese such as a Gloucester or a nice Wensleydale. But was not Darcy always right about everything? And why did the man not seem to find that exhausting? Bingley was only right about something a few times a day, and he slept well every night, tired from all the effort of thinking and deciding things correctly.

Unfortunately, now believing Bingley favoured Stilton, Cook had sought to please her new master by preparing a final course consisting entirely of apples and that vile cerulean substance. If he never ate another bite of the accursed cheesy comestible as long as he lived, he would be a happy man. Well, he already was a happy man; he had a new estate! So perhaps he could stomach more cheese if pressed to do so. Certainly, he would always be happy to eat cheese for his dear friend's sake, especially if, in doing so, he could help the poor fellow recover from an uncharacteristic slip-up concerning the man's favourite topic, Greek mythology.

Speaking of his new estate, Bingley realised he had not yet heard Darcy's opinion of it after their day appreciating its beauties.

"Say, Darcy, what say you of Netherfield Park now that you have seen it?"

Darcy flicked a piece of lint—or perhaps it was an errant crumb? That seemed unlikely since the man was a paragon of table manners; perhaps it was the result of Hurst's slovenly dining habits?—off his sleeve. Then he stood quietly, unmoving, seemingly barely breathing. He was in that statue-like pose Bingley most feared yet most admired. This brooding stillness was the essence of the man. Caroline was correct; it should be bottled! It would scare away any shufflers or jingle brains. Bingley waited another moment, but Darcy remained ponderous and silent. It was distracting, damn it, whenever Darcy thought deeply. Which was often. Bingley stared at him, idly debating the depth of his friend's chin cleft and wondered what was going on in that enormous brain of his.

"Darcy, you must share your opinion!"

Darcy pushed himself away from the mantel and sat in the chair across from the settee. Even seated, he seemed to tower over Bingley, who groaned quietly and sat up straighter.

"The house has decent bones, but there is serious work to be done on it and on the rest of the estate. It will take time, labour, and money."

How wonderful! Bingley was excited beyond measure. Here he was—he, Charles Bingley!—about to have a serious discussion with Darcy concerning the care and feeding of his very own, very real, estate! It was no fantastical figment of his imagination. Not this time. He tried to remember all the profound questions and knowing comments he had prepared based on his earlier, admittedly quite cursory, perusal of both—both!—*A Gentleman's Guide to Farming* and *Goats: A User's Manual*. Sadly, much of what he had read had slipped his mind since then, and the remainder of it now fled altogether. All he could remember was something about medicinal uses of goat milk and the benefits of machines for timely chaff cutting—whatever that meant!

Bingley nodded. "Well, yes. There are some stiles and fence posts that need rebuilding and replacing, and, um, the wall coverings are dreadfully out of date, and yes, the library is far too empty even for my tastes. But the land is good, and the house is well built. Also, drainage." There! He had managed to slip in the bit about drainage at the last minute. Hurrah!

Darcy did not hide a grimace. "The wall coverings are best left to your sisters. But yes, water is settled near the embankment behind the house, so you must address at least one drainage issue. Two or three chimneys require masons to repair them. The fields have not been given a proper rotation between oats and barley, and a few tenants' roofs and outbuildings are in poor condition. A considerable number of trees are dead or dying, which—"

"I see." Bingley waved his hand impatiently. "These problems are minor. I can address them with my steward."

"You have no steward, Bingley." Darcy leaned back. "Mr. Robson will assist you until we find one for Netherfield."

Ah yes, Darcy's steward was due to arrive within a se'nnight to appraise the estate. He was Darcy's right hand at Pemberley and had served the estate since the death of the elder Mr. Wickham. The "good" Mr. Wickham. A good man with a bad son. Some people were not so good. Some were cruel or angry. Every family had one or two of those. Not Darcy's, of course, although his cousins were a bit blustery. Caroline certainly thought so.

Bingley reflected on something he had overheard the serving girl—Nellie, was it?—say as she staggered away from the table holding the giant roast on a silver platter. Caroline and Louisa had been making a terrible fuss about the roast: it was undercooked or overcooked or perhaps it was the sauce or the garnish. Bingley was not really sure what they had been complaining about because he had not been paying attention. Instead, he had been admiring Darcy's fine table manners. Darcy really did have a way with a knife and fork, to say nothing of a spoon. But the maid had not noticed his skill with them. Oh no, her attention had been on the table's other occupants when she walked away, muttering, "Dreadful, dreadful women." And really, Bingley could not disagree, as much as it pained him to say so. His sisters *were* dreadful. They always had been.

He sprang out of his seat and strode to the liquor cabinet. "Say, Darcy, have I told you about the man I met when I was here a few weeks ago? Before I went to fetch you in London, that is." Bingley was keen to share the news of his conversation with his closest neighbour. He had even visited the man at his estate, Longbourn. Yes, he was off to an excellent start in his new neighbourhood! Not like that other time.

"No, I do not believe so."

"Ah! Well, Mr. Beignet, who owns the neighbouring estate, paid me a call."

Darcy frowned. "He is French?"

Bingley paused. "Why would you think that?" He poured two servings of port and handed one to Darcy, who smelt it warily.

"Oh, do not make a fuss!" Bingley cried with a hearty laugh. "Hurst was worried and brought bottles from his own stock."

Darcy leaned back in his chair and took a sip. His eyebrows rose appreciatively. Hurst would have been pleased had he been awake to see it.

"After Beignet paid a call, I returned it and visited him at Longbourn. His estate is a scarce three miles from my front door." Bingley smiled, pleased to have provided Darcy with a fact and figure about the neighbourhood. "You should see his library, man! It is positively jammed with books. Almost as many as you have at Pemberley. Though, come to think of it, his library is considerably smaller than yours." He stopped to think for a moment. "Well, perhaps much smaller. I would say he had somewhere between five and twenty and a hundred and fifty books. Give or take a hundred books."

"You did not ask the exact number?" Darcy gave him a droll look. "I am shocked by the oversight."

"Other numbers were far more interesting!" Bingley perched on the edge of the settee. "Beignet has five daughters! I did not meet any of them, but the neighbours said all but one, or perhaps two, are quite handsome."

Darcy's expression shifted quickly to one that was darker and thus far less pleasant for Bingley to rest his eyes upon—his tired eyes.

"Darcy, do be fair. We are new to the neighbourhood, and we must be pleasant and friendly to everyone. And there is nothing unpleasant about comely ladies. It speaks well of the town." He bit back a yawn. "If the cows we saw earlier are any indication, they should be beautiful indeed!"

"Cows?" Darcy's undignified snort was barely repressed. "The weathervanes and finely maintained lanes provide great reassurance that this bit of wilderness has the greatest beauties in all of England."

"As I left Longbourn," Bingley said quickly, wishing to return to the subject of ladies, "I caught a glimpse of one of the sisters, and she was admittedly plain, but she had great earnestness. And she was reading a book!"

"A book?" Darcy's gaze drifted about the room and its lonely bookshelves.

"I told you Mr. Beignet has a fine collection of books." Bingley yawned and, still clutching his glass, stretched out his arms. "All this riding about in the countryside is tiring."

"Perhaps you are a man better meant for town life." Darcy set his glass on the table and crossed his legs, clearly not at all fatigued.

Bingley sat up a little straighter and swallowed a yawn. "I am decided on Netherfield. The house and land suit me, the people are pleasant, and the nice little shops are as fine as those in London." At Darcy's incredulous laugh, he quickly added, "Nearly so, if one is looking for country things!"

"A gentleman may avoid London's heat and stench in the summer, but not all truly enjoy the country. They miss their entertainments, their clubs, the theatre." Darcy steepled his fingers, a sure sign he was posing an important question. "You will not regret spending these weeks sitting at a desk or managing repairs and settling tenant disagreements?"

"No!" Bingley cried. "It is time for me to do as my father hoped and begin this new step in my life." He took a large swallow of port. "There is much to occupy and amuse me and my sisters and our guests. Have I mentioned there is to be an assembly?"

Darcy stared at him blankly.

"In two days' time! There you will meet the kind people of Meryton and Mr. Beignet and his seven handsome daughters!"

"Five—and not all may be handsome." Darcy shook his head. "I think not. There will be nothing and no one to tempt me here, and my appearance at such a gathering would draw attention and expectations among these families and their daughters."

"Your appearance? You are my guest, as is Hurst. We all wear cravats and comb our hair, and we will be equals to my neighbours."

"They are country strangers," Darcy growled.

"You sound like Caroline, you know," Bingley said blearily. Caught by yet another yawn, he closed his eyes and missed Darcy's startled expression. "Please do not be awful; you are my best friend."

Darcy shifted in his chair and sighed quietly. He watched Bingley drift off to sleep in that familiar and enviable way of the young, innocent, or simple-minded. The empty tumbler fell from Bingley's hand and rolled towards Darcy's boots.

"And you are mine," he said quietly as he rose to his feet and retrieved the glass. "What small cost is a night amid strangers in their country best?"

He looked up when the door opened and watched a footman as he examined and refilled the decanters to ensure there was still enough liquor in them to addle a man's brains.

"See to it that Miss Bingley is told we shall not re-join the ladies this evening, and have her brother deposited in the master's quarters."

He departed gloomily, reflecting on the tedium awaiting him at the forthcoming assembly. Dreadful local folk, ugly girls. No doubt it would be the worst day, maybe the worst month, of his life.

Part II: Verum Etiam Amicum Qui Intuctur, Tamquam Exemplar Aliquod Intuetur Sui

He Who Looks Upon a True Friend Looks, As It Were, Upon a Better Image of Himself

The house—*his* house!—was far too quiet. All the joy and happiness that once filled it had fled along with the Bennets' carriage. It was difficult to believe that two days had passed since their departure! His angel was gone from Netherfield—risen from her sickbed and returned to Longbourn. The relief in Bingley's stomach, which had been tied in worried knots during her illness, warred with the ache in his heart from her absence. He wondered which would win as his stomach had the advantage in speed and size whilst his heart was superior in strength and durability.

Miss Jane Bennet was perfection: kind, considerate, and graceful in her features and manners. And utterly beautiful. Now she was no longer under his roof and his protection, her goodness mere steps away. Three miles was too far from his duelling stomach and heart!

The company she left behind was much less perfect than she. Caroline showed undisguised joy when the carriage pulled away; Louisa appeared as pleased by the empty chambers as she was by the freedom to speak freely. Hurst was no help either, having fallen asleep only a few minutes into Bingley's reflections regarding the Bennets' departure. It was a pity, really, since Hurst began to snore just as Bingley gained his second wind.

In contrast to the comatose Hurst, Darcy had become increasingly restless. For two days now, he had paced and stamped about, adjusting his cuffs and looking disapprovingly out the window. One by one, he had taken out each of the six books from the shelf in Bingley's study and set about reading it, barely managing thirty seconds before slamming the book shut and returning it to its place, muttering what sounded like "ridiculous excuse for a library." Bingley knew his library compared poorly with the glory that was Pemberley's, but six books—*seven* if you counted the novel hidden under the cushion in the window seat—was a beginning. Besides, Darcy had brought a box of books to Netherfield, thick volumes full of Latin, French, and German words. It was not Bingley's fault that his friend was tired of his own books and toys, though it did reflect poorly on his ability as a host to entertain his guest. He never found life dull when he was at one of Darcy's houses. There were savoury meals, attentive servants, speedy horses, happy dogs—

Oh! Dogs! Netherfield needed dogs! Dogs to sit at his feet while he stared into the fire, thinking deep thoughts and making plans for his lands. Dogs to chase after him when he rode out on his horse and to lick his hand, joyful to see him home safely. Miss Bennet loved dogs. He had once seen her staring adoringly at a pup on the high street in Meryton. Why had he not taken the pup into his home? Oh, if only he had a dog here now to cheer up Darcy.

He was amazed to see his normally composed friend so agitated. There was nothing for it really. When this rain passed, he must take Darcy out for an afternoon gallop and allow him to release some of his manly energy, of which he currently seemed to have an abundance. Secretly, Bingley hoped they might also have a chance encounter with one or more of the Bennet sisters if they were out and about in the neighbourhood.

Sadly, the two men had not been as fortunate earlier that day when they rode in the direction of Longbourn, nor when they loitered about some stiles not far from that house and examined a thicket of particularly fine shrubbery that fortuitously offered a clear line of sight to the road to town. Bingley hoped Darcy had not noticed his frequent glances in that direction. He was quite certain his friend had not, though, since Bingley had done it so stealthily. Finally, after Darcy appeared impatient with his questions about leaves and twigs, he resigned himself that he would not see his angel. He and Darcy turned their horses towards Meryton, Bingley lagging a bit behind in despair.

And then, just there in the middle of the muddy, dung-strewn high street, his angel had appeared as though lit by a shaft of golden light! He was sure that bells had rung as well; though it was possible it was only the church bells calling the faithful to prayer. How fortunate! It was as if it was meant to be. His horse flew like one of Cupid's arrows right to Miss Bennet's side where he hallooed her with great enthusiasm. He could not resist mentioning that he and Darcy had been on their way to Longbourn to see the sisters although it was quite clear they had come from the opposite direction altogether.

Darcy seemed not to share his assessment that this chance encounter was so auspicious, however. Far from partaking in Bingley's delight at the meeting, he appeared to think it was awful. Actually, it was quite peculiar; Darcy had displayed the most violently rude manners! One moment, he was nodding politely to the Bennet sisters, and the next, he was charging off on his horse. Bingley was not certain Darcy had even exchanged words with anyone before suddenly taking off as if stung by a wasp or struck by the urgent need for a cup of tea and a biscuit. These were the things that usually set Bingley charging off, but he had not been paying enough attention to Darcy to know whether either of these was the cause. How could he occupy himself with Darcy's business when Miss Bennet was near?

But who were those men who had been talking to the sisters? Some of them wore uniforms while at least one of them—the man with his back to

Bingley—did not. Was it the red coats that upset Darcy, perhaps reminding him of his cousin, the rather overwhelming Colonel Fitzwilliam? Was the colonel on the Continent, spying or fighting or doing some such dangerous thing? Likely, Darcy was full of unspoken worry for him. Of course, it would be unspoken as Darcy never shared his concerns with anyone, at least not with Bingley.

He must ensure that Darcy knew he was a good and faithful listener in whom he could place total trust. Such was the mark of true friendship—as well as a good trait in a dog. A large dog with jaunty ears and a wagging tail. But first, he must ask Darcy whether he knew those men…and whether Jane was in any danger from their attentions!

Sadly, Bingley had not yet been able to put any queries to his estimable friend. He had not seen him since their return to Netherfield when Darcy left his steaming horse in the stable and disappeared into his rooms. Now it was teatime, and he still had not put in an appearance.

"Where is Darcy?" Hurst strolled through the door to the study and settled himself in one of the aged, oversized chairs that Caroline despised but had yet to replace. It would be a shame when they were gone. Ugly they might be, with swirling fabric patterns resembling skulls and lobster claws, but they were remarkably comfortable for napping. "This house lacks sense when he is not standing about, still and silent."

"He is in his chambers." Bingley heaved a tremendous sigh and slumped a bit in his own skull-and-lobster chair. Hurst was correct. A room without Darcy was indeed lonely and lacking sense. Even the tea on the table seemed unsatisfactory although the plum tart's crust had a pleasing look about it.

"Ah, hiding from Caroline, writing more letters, or brooding over something some ancient Greek did in the Peloponnesian War?"

"None of the above," came an irritated voice from the doorway. "The Punic Wars merit deeper consideration, however."

"Darcy!" Bingley jumped to his feet as his friend entered the room. "At last, you are come. We are in dire need of music, laughter, and conversation!"

"There has been no music here in days," Darcy replied darkly. "And a storm is on its way."

A storm indeed. Bingley watched as the man folded his arms and stared out at the darkening sky. He wondered whether Darcy's mood was affected by the damp weather or perhaps a sudden, overwhelming, peckish feeling such as the one he himself was currently experiencing. Or did Darcy find the house as sad and empty as Bingley did now that the Bennet sisters were gone? Miss Bennet's goodness had permeated more than his heart, he realised. His angel's kindness and bewitching beauty had left a spell on Netherfield and its inhabitants. Contemplating Miss Bennet's pulchritude, Bingley absently poured Darcy a cup of tea.

"Would you care for some refreshments?" Bingley asked Darcy, holding the beverage out to him. "Or a ginger biscuit? Miss Elizabeth told her maid they were a favourite of her sister's."

"O-ho!" Hurst cried. "Did you take notes? What is her *least* favourite?" He laughed merrily in spite of Bingley's annoyed glance. He must give Hurst a cup too, and as quickly as possible, to make him stop prattling on in this absurd way. But first, Darcy must have his tea, of course!

When Darcy did not reach for the offered cup, Bingley took a closer look and noticed that his friend's hand was curled into a fist, which was a bit peculiar given they were not in a boxing establishment. It was even odder that the fist was marred by a most curious discolouration. A bruise? A scrape? Perhaps it was the *literal* mark of a true gentleman, and Bingley had simply never noticed it before? If anyone might have one of those, it would be Darcy! Ha ha! Maybe Bingley could get a tattoo to match at one of those places down by the docks where sailors congregated. He and Darcy could be like brothers! On second thought, getting a tattoo sounded rather painful, involving as it did India ink, rusty nails, and sea turtle tusks or whatnot. However, upon further examination, the mark on Darcy's hand was clearly not a tattoo but some kind of injury, as Bingley had originally suspected. Poor fellow.

"What have you done to your hand, Darcy? Did you hold the reins too tightly or perhaps punch the wall or some such nonsense?" Bingley laughed heartily. His friend would never do that. He handled his disappointments and frustrations much better than Bingley did. Darcy was never one to stomp on his hat, scold a spider on the wall most severely, or sneeze more loudly than was absolutely necessary in a fit of pique. He held everything in admirably, expertly suppressing his feelings in such a gentlemanly manner that Bingley could hardly tell whether he had any feelings at all. In point of fact, did Darcy ever *have* disappointments and frustrations? Bingley felt ashamed at even having *thought* about fists hitting walls in conjunction with his genteel friend.

"What? Certainly not," Darcy snapped, rubbing the offending spot as if he could erase it by force of will. "Why would you ask me such a thing?"

Hurst snorted loudly in that rudely ridiculous manner he paraded about in company. "Did you discover Caroline in your rooms again and hurt your hand slamming the door? Or did you have to knock her out to make your escape?" Then he raised his hand to his chest like a Roman centurion. "I salute you."

"You think ill of your sister and of me, Hurst." Lifting his uninjured hand, Darcy took the proffered cup from Bingley and shrugged. "I scraped my hand on my trunk searching for a book."

Ah, a book accident. Now *that* made sense. Feeling reassured about his friend's disposition, Bingley eased himself back into his lobster chair. Darcy chose to stand by the mantelpiece, apparently his newest favourite haunt. He rubbed the side of his long, elegant neck. Bingley wondered whether the man's hives were flaring up again. Or perhaps the book accident had somehow affected that area as well.

"I wish Miss Bennet and Miss Elizabeth were here," Bingley said, then hastily added, "In good health, of course. Jane, um, Miss Bennet brightened the house with her beauty, and Miss Elizabeth is so clever." Met with silence from one man and the sound of slurping from the other, he addressed the former. "Darcy, I know you were pleased to see Caroline matched—or even overmatched—by Miss Elizabeth's wits. Rarely, have I seen my sister so vexed."

Darcy's eyebrow—the right one, as always—rose slightly.

"Did you not think so, Darcy?"

"Your sister has long enjoyed a superiority of mind and a quickness in conversation while in London society," Darcy said in a brisk voice whilst setting his tea down on the mantelpiece. "Meeting a young lady of equal ability, and in the country no less, has been an unexpected…event."

"Event?" Hurst made another of those noises certain to attract notice in a public gathering as he pulled out his flask and surreptitiously poured some brandy into his tea. "I say, Darcy, watching Miss Elizabeth make sport of my sister has been far more entertaining than anything I have seen in months at White's or Angelo's."

"Oh, Miss Elizabeth was certainly a match for Caroline, but Miss Bennet's conversation was of equal merit," Bingley cried. "Darcy, did you not admire Miss Bennet when she spoke to me at length about the drainage problems at Netherfield? It seems her father's property has drainage issues as well!"

"Imagine that," drawled Hurst. "Who could have guessed you two would have so much in common? Perhaps Beignet can give you some pointers about water tables and overflow."

"Oh no, indeed!" Bingley exclaimed, waving his delicious ginger biscuit in the air. Perhaps he should have another one. "I mean her father no disrespect, but Darcy is the real expert on drainage. I shall rely on his good judgment in all things drainage related." He popped the last of the biscuit into his mouth.

"Just wait till you hear what he has to say about crop rotation," Hurst interjected, leaning further back into his chair.

Darcy scowled at him. "Bennet. The last name is Bennet."

Bingley swallowed and nodded. "Yes, quite so. Miss Bennet truly seemed quite taken with my ideas about gravel and ditches. Well, they were really Darcy's ideas, but I did wonder…do you think she fancies me? She looked at me *just so*…" Bingley looked eagerly back and forth between Hurst and Darcy.

"Perhaps she was merely being polite, Bingley," Darcy said in an unusually gentle tone. "Most young ladies have no care for ditches and gravel."

Bingley looked up at his friend, so occupied with his big, busy life, his estates, and his dear sister, yet always full of concern for him, the son of a tradesman just embarking on the life of a landed gentleman. Darcy knew more than anyone else about ditches and gravel, but he was sensitive to the fact that others might not find them terribly interesting. He would never be derisive of a young lady's opinions. Look at his lively debates with Miss Elizabeth in those conversations that no one else understood. Even Caroline had been confused.

"Did you and Miss Elizabeth discuss ditches and gravel? Your conversations were rather difficult to follow."

Darcy gave him an incredulous look. His cheeks reddened, nearly matching that mark on his hand.

"You were discussing the requirements of being an accomplished woman! I admit I did not hear every word—I was preoccupied with worry for Miss Bennet's ill health—nor did I understand the parts in Latin, but surely the knowledge of crop rotation and gravel usage might have been canvassed!"

"We spoke not a word in Latin, Bingley." Darcy peered closely at him, his dark eyes narrowed in apparent exasperation. "Nor of anything to do with managing estates."

"Your Miss Jane Beignet is as sweet as a sugarplum, with the light and airy carriage of spun sugar and the beauty of a whipped syllabub, yet her sister is best compared to a mud pie?" Hurst shook his head. "Badly done, Bingley. Surely, Miss Elizabeth is conversant with topics beyond mud and manure."

Darcy cleared his throat. "Marzipan, perhaps?" He sipped his tea and stared out the window.

"Oh yes, marzipan." Hurst chortled and sank deeper into his seat. "A serving of sweetmeat, that Beignet, with an extra dusting of sugar."

"Bennet!" Bingley cried. "Their name is Bennet, and they are not to be compared to baked goods!" His teacup clattered down onto the saucer where it perched unsteadily close to the edge.

"Or puddings?"

Bingley's jaw dropped. He looked to Darcy, expecting him to share in his indignation, but found him looking amused at Hurst's joke. He was shocked. Darcy was a gentleman, and as much as he might wish to complain about Bingley's sisters and call them rude, presumptuous, or awful, he did not. He certainly had never said their names and that of a sweet treat in the same sentence! What had gotten into the man, and why did he prefer Hurst's conversation to his own?

Very well, he must refrain from discussing drainage. It was dull, and Darcy disliked dull conversation with dull people. Simple enough. No dull friends or relations for Darcy, only dull books.

Feeling unequal to the topic of dull books and irritated that Hurst would compare Miss Bennet to a sugarplum, Bingley wracked his brain for a new subject of discussion. Ah, yes! Those men in the street who were talking to his angel and her sisters. Could *they* be the reason that Darcy had shot back to Netherfield so abruptly? It was difficult to imagine why. More likely was that Darcy had stepped in something unspeakable and wanted to prevent the ladies from being offended by the substance, whatever it was, on his fine boots. The more he thought about it, though, the more convinced he became that it was the men and not the odious animal, vegetable, or mineral matter on his Hessians that caused Darcy to depart so precipitously. Repugnant substances would not dare stick to that gentleman's soles.

"Darcy," he said offhandedly, "those men we saw speaking to the Miss Bennets, do you know them?"

As soon as the words left his mouth, Bingley wished he could swallow them right back in. Darcy was worried about his cousin fighting on the Continent, and it would not do to remind him of it by speaking of soldiers. Well, one could not take back the words one had already spoken, could one? He had learned this the hard way from that time with…what was her name? Oh yes, Miss Fothergill. And indeed, he saw Darcy's broad and heroic shoulders tense at his question. The poor man, so terribly anxious about his cousin. It was commendable how much he cared for his family, even that rapscallion, the colonel. How could he jolly the man out of his distress?

"I would rather not speak of it," Darcy intoned in his most commanding master-of-Pemberley voice.

"Oh, come now," Bingley teased, pocketing a biscuit in his waistcoat for later. "I am sure it is nothing as bad as all that. You have only just met them. What could they have done? Importuned you for money? Insulted your horse?" Bingley rummaged around in his head for the most preposterous, the most ludicrous, the most absurd suggestion imaginable. "Asked you for Georgiana's hand in marriage?" He laughed heartily. Such a ridiculous proposition. Georgiana was only fifteen years old, after all.

Darcy froze. Stiffly, he said, "What on earth would possess you to say such a thing, Bingley, even in jest?"

Oh dear. Perhaps one of them had indeed insulted Darcy's horse. Bingley had no idea that Darcy could become so expressive about his equine companion since he rarely became expressive about anything. In the future, Bingley must remember to tread carefully when it came to Darcy's fine steed.

"Is Aeschylus well?" Bingley asked solicitously.

"Why are we speaking of my horse?" Darcy looked both confused and relieved.

"Would you rather speak of the delectable Beignet sisters?" came Hurst's voice from his recumbent position on the settee, *Bingley's* settee, where he had somehow stealthily moved without Bingley's notice. Hurst was faster than he looked. Now his feet were most unbecomingly situated on the settee's arm, his head on a cushion at the other end. Bingley had never before had an opinion one way or the other about the propriety of putting one's feet on the furniture, but he found he had strong convictions about it now that it was *his* settee. One never knew where those feet had been, especially given Hurst's shocking habits.

"Do not be offensive, Hurst, with your allusions to cakes and puddings." Darcy pushed off the mantelpiece and stalked over to Bingley's desk to set down his cup and saucer with less gentleness than annoyance. "As to your enquiry, Bingley, Aeschylus is quite well. Your stable is stocked with hay and oats, and the stable hand is capable of meeting his needs."

Bingley's stomach made an unspeakably loud noise, and his face reddened.

"Hay and oats beget an appetite where sugar buns and blancmange do not?" Hurst's eyebrows rose. "This new house of yours is producing such unexpected disclosures. Have *you* any to share, Darcy?"

Darcy rubbed his chin and stared off towards the windows. "I am a private man, but I hide no secrets." He turned to Bingley. "I am acquainted with one of the men we saw in Meryton, as are you. He is no friend of mine nor should he be a friend to you."

Bingley gasped, and immediately hoped Hurst would not comment on it. Such a statement to make about another gentleman…another man. Darcy most decidedly did not refer to him as a gentleman. "I know him? His name? Will you tell me his name and the reason—?"

"It was George Wickham."

No! Not the terrible, no-good, awful man whose name and slight height advantage made Darcy scowl even more than was his usual wont. Not here, of all the towns in all of England!

Darcy turned quickly and strode to the door. Poor man. First his cousin fighting on the Continent, then his horse, and now Wickham. What a dreadful day it had been for him. His burdens were heavy indeed.

"I have letters to write. Until this evening, gentlemen." Darcy disappeared into the hall, and they listened to the fading sound of his boots clicking on the wood floor.

"Oh my!" Bingley laid his head back in his chair. "Wickham! The man Darcy most disdains for reasons never fully explained. I shall hope not to meet him again in any society we share in Meryton…that is, if it is possible to exclude a member of the militia."

"Caroline knows all about exclusion from society. Ask her." Hurst's increasingly languid voice and manner left Bingley with the distinct impression that the man would soon slip entirely down between the settee's cushions, possibly never to be seen again.

Bingley glared at Hurst before letting out a deep, disappointed sigh. "Darcy has fled our company."

"Your company, not mine," Hurst mumbled, yawning. "He and I are perfectly good friends. Perhaps you should not jump about so madly in your conversations, Bingley. It is both dull and exhausting." He closed his eyes.

Bingley inhaled a great gust of air in preparation for making a brilliant retort but instead watched, fascinated, as his brother slid slowly into a deep, open-mouthed slumber.

The steadily increasing rain dampened his mood as it washed away the chance for another ride in search of Jane Bennet. But the sound of raindrops was soothing, so very soothing. Hurst looked so extraordinarily comfortable snoring away that it made his own eyes grow heavy. Bingley sighed and rested his head against the wing of his chair. The swirling lobsters were close to his eyes, their blue and maroon claws flooding his vision. His arms slid off the chair and knocked his teacup to the soft carpet. He dreamt of crustaceans.

Part III: Certum Est Quia Impossible Est

It Is Certain Because It Is Impossible

It was not just Darcy who was an awful object on a Sunday night. London in January was a big fat yawn, and Bingley knew exactly who deserved the blame: Darcy. And Caroline. And maybe Jane Bennet. No! He would not think of *her*. He needed to focus on the here and now—the *here* being Darcy's study and the *now* being this moment when he had nothing whatsoever to do.

Yes, London was dull, dull, dull.

There were no women, no clubs, and no horses, cockfights, or pugilistic contests to catch the fancy of a restless young man. Bingley had often imagined himself as a man about town, a well-liked man who knew how to enjoy himself and the amusements afforded by a fat purse and the dropping of the right name. He liked to think that he, Charles Horatio Bingley, could lead the merry life that Darcy rejected in favour of his dusty books and tiresome ancient maps. Blasted maps. Who knew old paper was so brittle? Darcy should have warned him. And then there were those museums and the endless collecting. Snowflakes, was it, this month? Or was Darcy still pocketing stones, straw plaits, and chestnuts as he had last autumn at Netherfield?

Since closing his country house and returning to the social whirl of the *ton*, Bingley had found himself at odds with the demands of his sisters and annoyed with the short stack of cards deposited on his desk every day. There should be more. More cards, more calls, more opportunities for fun. Usually he could count on Darcy to accompany him, however reluctantly, on his forays into society, and Bingley hated to do anything alone. Having Darcy as company always brightened the evening. Everyone was pleased to see the master of Pemberley, and seeing *him* made them see *Bingley* in the ways Caroline insisted he needed to be seen. To his credit, Darcy never behaved as though he was simply doing a duty to his friend. In fact, most of the time the great man seemed to enjoy himself on their social excursions.

But Darcy of late was quite a bottle-head. His conversation was stiff, and his mind was off somewhere that Bingley could not fathom. All his energy seemed driven to his fingers, which he tapped incessantly on the table, his book, or a chair. Darcy's hands needed some other occupation. Bingley levelled a serious look at his most admirable friend. Fitzwilliam Darcy was a handsome man, but his profile was now marred by a furrowed brow and a steady frown. His hands, which could clench a steed's reins as powerfully as they wielded the steely shaft of a sword, were capable of much more than that irritating drumming.

God, the thinking, the musing, the turning over of a thought or a word. What had happened to his friend since they had left Hertfordshire? There, Darcy had been diverted from his family troubles or estate issues or whatever it was that had him so distraught last summer. At Netherfield, he had once again been spirited on his horse, accurate with his billiards cue, and animated during his conversations...well, mostly those with Miss Elizabeth. Ah, Elizabeth Bennet and those fine eyes. But it was better they were away from those Bennet sisters, no? Lovely as Jane Bennet might be—and she was very, very, very pretty—Bingley now recognised that her company was far less engaging than that of his tall, stoic friend. She was too quiet, demure, placid. So angelic yet not at all encouraging! And her sister was a bit too familiar, perhaps a bit too threatening to Darcy's equanimity. Better that it was just the two of them again.

Yes, indeed, no thinking. Thinking was a bad business. They needed a night out, just the two of them, enjoying manly pursuits with no such distractions.

But how to wrest Darcy away from his fascinations? The man was endlessly in the corner, staring into the darkness out the window or at the curtain or the wall. Come to think of it, he had not seen any sign of animation in Darcy since they had departed Hertfordshire. The last time he had seen his handsome friend show a dash of enthusiasm was, hmm…well, as had occurred to him just a moment before, most likely in conversation with Miss Elizabeth Bennet. Not that he had been paying close attention—no, not at all. But those two had spent considerable time speaking of books and poets and making comments in Latin, Greek, Italian, or some such jibber-jabber. Give him good old English any day!

At times, Bingley had noted that both Darcy and Miss Elizabeth had flared nostrils while spouting gibble-gabble at each other. Not that he had paid too much attention; he had had other things on his mind. Were they angry, or did all that nostril flaring denote some other emotion? It had certainly *appeared* to be anger. But why were they so heated if they were only discussing dry old books?

He had not seen such a look on Darcy's face since that time back at Cambridge when the serving girl had touched his... Bingley flushed. Oh, Darcy would hate that he remembered it so clearly. Yet it had led to the most illuminating conversation of his young life in which his older friend had haltingly explained how proper consummation worked: what part went where and when, and the way tongues might be involved, but that he must nevertheless always remember that it was not proper to touch even a young lady's ungloved hand until marriage. Bingley had had many questions about how the lips moved and where the noses were placed while kissing, and then Wickham had strolled in and laughed at him—at both of them, actually. That had prompted Darcy's nostrils to flare as well, though in that instance, it clearly *had* been an expression of anger.

What had happened to his dear friend that he would argue about books with a kind-hearted, book-reading, country girl? Bingley did not understand how a person could become angry about a *book* of all things. And he found it perplexing that, even though Darcy had been angry with Miss Elizabeth, he had done something Bingley had never known him to do before: he had asked the lady to dance a reel! In the sitting room! Now *that* was odd.

But what was even more peculiar was that Miss Elizabeth had refused him. At least that seemed to be the case; he was not completely certain since he had been otherwise occupied in thinking of Jane—Miss Bennet—lying ill in her bed upstairs. Anyone could see that Darcy was all a gentleman should be, yet Miss Elizabeth had not seemed to appreciate it. Darcy had a fine mind, in fact a brilliant mind as far as Bingley could tell, honed by the finest education money could buy. He was the best master to his dependents, the best brother, the most loyal friend, the most accomplished sportsman, and was furthermore the owner of the broadest shoulders and the best seat Bingley had ever seen. And he had that which Bingley coveted most for himself—a cleft chin. How could Miss Elizabeth not see these things? Why had she argued with Darcy, who had such impeccable and widely appreciated discernment? It really was quite strange.

Well, Miss Elizabeth may not have understood Darcy's superiority of character, but Bingley was no fool. He knew what was what. Therefore, when Darcy had given Bingley his honest opinion of her elder sister, he had listened. Yes, Jane Bennet was all that was lovely, sweet, and gentle, and Bingley had thought that maybe... But Darcy had superb judgment in all things. He *must* have been right in his assessment that Miss Bennet's feelings had not truly been engaged. Anyway, Bingley was not really sad about the end of the affair. Things were likely better this way. It was back to being just Darcy and Bingley again as it always had been, and as it always would be, no matter what feminine distractions came their way.

And that brought him back to his original thought: how to persuade Darcy to stop stewing and have some fun. How could Bingley turn his friend's attention from these aimless avenues of contemplation and get him over to Almack's or, even better, to that club his imposing moustachioed cousin boasted about when in his cups? Which was quite often if one thought about what was actually proper for an officer and a gentleman. Ah, to be the son of an earl.

Nevertheless, perhaps temporary temptations of the feminine kind were not quite the thing. Darcy was a private man. Bingley did not know whether his proper, handsome friend had ever accompanied his cousin on those nocturnal visits to the French houses. In fact, he was not completely certain that Darcy had enjoyed the favours of *any* woman. He certainly had not had his heart touched; Bingley was sure of that.

But this was Fitzwilliam Tiberius Darcy! Of course he must have *known* women; though to Bingley's chagrin, his friend was an insufferably proper man who simply would neither celebrate nor share such information. Yet it was obvious that Darcy *could* enjoy many favours if he wished to, and he likely had done so. The ladies of the *ton*—be they married, widowed, hard-eyed or dewy fresh, in the marriage mart or spinster—were all endlessly batting their eyelashes at him and lowering their bodices and touching his sleeve. Not that Bingley was paying close attention, but people did talk. His sisters talked quite a bit, more than necessary, actually, and he had been made aware that Darcy was a much-admired, much-sought-after gentleman in possession of everything but a wife. He was an enigma, a man who confessed nothing of a personal nature to his particular friend. He talked instead of his travels, his books, his woods, and his sister. He fenced, he played his violin, and he did not fall asleep during Shakespeare. He was busy, important, and oh so interesting—at least he used to be.

Bingley drained his glass and trained a contemplative eye on his friend. What, exactly, was he about? Why was he brooding and sighing heavily, sipping his brandy and staring into the flames? On an excruciatingly dull Sunday night when they could have been doing something *much* more entertaining? One would think he was in pain from an aching tooth or a sore toe!

"Darcy, old man! What do you say we step out this evening? What has you so down at the mouth? Some fresh air—that is what you need!"

The great man slowly turned his head and gazed at him. "Bingley, it is the Sabbath. Moreover, it is near dark and near dinner, not to mention it is snowing outside. What could possibly claim our attention in this supposed fresh air?"

In an effort to divert Darcy's attention while he organised his thoughts in reply to the man's always-irrefutable logic, Bingley bounced across the room and seized the poker from the fireplace. He leaned over and stabbed at a log, sending sparks up the chimney and compelling a teary cough from his friend.

"Good God, Bingley! Sit down and put that thing away!" Darcy raised a handkerchief and wiped at his eyes.

Hmm. A remarkably lacy bit of cloth. From a lady friend? Aha! He could make out some initials in the corner. Was that an E? Or perhaps a Q? "Sorry, Darcy. Um, that handkerchief is a fine piece of work. Was it a gift?"

He poured a generous serving of brandy into Darcy's glass and then filled his own empty one.

Darcy glared at him and rather quickly stuffed the cloth into his pocket. "For heaven's sake, Bingley. Are you so at loose ends that you wish to discuss linens and embroidery?" He raised his glass to his lips and took a large draught.

"Oh, well. It is just, you see...you have been quiet since our return to town. I did not know whether you had regretted our leaving?" Bingley gulped and took a deep swallow of the brandy, wondering why Darcy was staring at him curiously. He hastened to interject, "Not that I regret it...not in the least." Why was Darcy so quick to anger with him? He and Miss Elizabeth had exchanged sharp, clever words, and he had never seemed quite as angry with her. Perhaps Bingley should use bigger words?

"Me? Regret leaving a one-stable village to return to my comfortable home and visit my sister for the holiday season? I think not."

Bingley sank down into the chair across from his friend. "Why, then, have you been so little out and about? Caroline was disappointed not to find you at the Altons' ball." He raised his eyebrows suggestively. "And she was not the only young lady left with disappointed hopes."

He caught a sudden, momentary glimpse of something peculiar on Darcy's face, gone as soon as he noticed it. Pain? That seemed unlikely. "Yes, well. We all have our duties," Darcy said. "I cannot attend *every* ball."

Bingley wished to cry out that *he* would attend every ball had he the good fortune and birthright to do so. *Every* ball! He would reply to every card, every invitation, pleasing himself as well as his sisters. Darcy's choice not to do so was singular—and rather sad. How could any man be weary of gaiety?

Instead, he shook his head as though he understood such responsibilities. "I see. If dancing and eluding matchmaking matrons is not to your taste, perhaps we could petition your cousin to take us over to that house he favours…?"

Bingley trailed off, unable to look Darcy in the eye. There, he had boldly mentioned it! But did he really want to go to one of those houses? He had been to such a place but once, when his uncle deposited his nineteen-year-old self on a courtesan's doorstep and announced he would expect a timely report on his experience. Bingley had managed to stammer his way through a brief summary the next day, then fled to his rooms and swore to himself that he would never ever again bed a raven-haired woman. She had left marks on his person with her lips and teeth! A minx, she was—a vixen, that Mademoiselle Angélique!

Oh no, he had not said her name aloud just now, had he? Just to make certain, he glanced up at Darcy, who fortunately remained quiet with his eyes fixed on the fire. Bingley wiped his hand across his mouth in relief. Then he suddenly realised Darcy was answering his question. What had it been again?

"Bingley, I have no flames to quench, no desire to seek comfort in the arms of a well-practised but ill-educated woman."

"Very well!" Bingley replied happily, all thoughts of dark-haired women blessedly swept from his brain as he delighted in pondering the mischief the two of them could get into even if they had to stay here at Darcy's rather than going out. Perhaps he could tease his companion into a better mood through the careful application of copious amounts of spirits. "More brandy, my friend?"

And so they drank. At first with some restraint and then with increasing vigour. The deeper they drank, the more the warmth of Darcy's fine liquor loosened their tongues. Plates of cold meats and cheeses arrived, but they were disregarded. Before long, the two young men found themselves sprawled side by side in their respective leather armchairs separated by the decanter on a little table and exchanging confidences such as they never had before.

"What is it you like about that Miss Elizabeth Bennet?" Bingley mumbled, gesturing with his brandy glass. "Truly, I cannot account for it. Yes, she has pretty eyes, and she certainly had Caroline's measure, but still…"

"Well, she is completely unsuitable for a man of my consequence. But I will admit that I enjoyed sparring with her."

"Sparring?" Bingley sputtered. "*We* spar! I hope you were not actually thinking about engaging in fisticuffs with the lady." He made little punches with his fists and slopped his brandy on the carpet.

Darcy grimaced at his wet rug and looked at his friend with mingled pity and fondness. "I did not mean *literal* sparring. *Verbal* sparring." He sighed and quietly added, "With tongues, not hands."

Bingley nodded, listing a bit. "Ah, naturally. Still, what do you need *her* for, man? You have me for that. Is that not what our gentleman friends are for?"

"Bingley, be serious." The ratio of pity to fondness in Darcy's expression increased substantially. "It is hardly the same sort of—"

"No, truly. You like to discuss, hmm…Herodotus, right? All right, then. I read Herodotus at Cambridge just as you did. Say something clever about Herodotus. I shall argue with you." Bingley sat up as straight as he could and adopted a serious mien. In spite of his best efforts, he still leaned to the right a bit.

Darcy eyed him with considerable scepticism. "Very well. Let us discuss Herodotus's enduring argument with his famous contemporary, Thomas Aquinas, on the nature of being and on the precise number of angels who could dance on the head of a pin."

Bingley nodded vigorously, and he regretted it almost immediately. "Yes, exactly so. This is just the sort of thing I meant. Please remind me: How many angels did each man say?"

Darcy slumped back in his chair, slapping his glass down on the silver tray between them. "For God's sake, man. Herodotus lived in the fifth century before Christ while Thomas Aquinas lived a mere six hundred years prior to our own time. They never disagreed about this or anything else for that matter."

Bingley flushed to the tips of his already-red ears. "Then what, may I ask, was your intention in proposing such a ridiculous topic for discussion?"

Darcy rubbed his hand across his jaw. "You wished to have an intellectual debate. I attempted to ascertain whether you were prepared do so. Perhaps we are more evenly matched for a game of darts." Evidently noting his friend's unsteadiness, he added gently, "Or billiards."

Bingley shrugged and tugged off his cravat. He leaned back in his chair. "Ladies wear skirts and are no good at riding, billiards, or darts. They are pretty things to look at though."

"Ladies are good for much more than admiration from afar."

"Ha ha! But a man does like to keep his distance, does he not?"

"Why do you say that?" asked Darcy, frowning. He leaned over and pulled off his boots. Always fastidious, even when more than a little intoxicated, he placed the boots carefully just under the table between the two chairs.

"Well, certainly one wants to stay away from Caroline and Louisa!"

"Yes, yes, one does, certainly." Darcy seemed to immediately think better of this and quickly continued, "I say that with the greatest respect, of course." But Bingley was not offended in any case. He knew they were dreadful. They always had been.

"If one were to judge all women by my sisters, one would think they are a fearsome lot. Such sharp tongues, such malice aforethought, such scheming and planning. Is it not better to maintain a proper distance and simply admire them from afar?"

Darcy thought about this for a moment, apparently measuring his response carefully. "I suppose it is if one judged all women by your sisters. But imagine for a moment what would happen if we considered other women we have known, women who exercise discernment and rationality."

Bingley shook his head. "I have never known such a woman."

"Have you never thought that this is because you have always kept your distance? Certainly, you can tell me much about the countenance, dress, and manners of numerous women, women with whom you have considered yourself in love. But can you say any more about them?"

"Oh yes. I do enjoy looking at them. They are quite beautiful, lovely, charming, and decorative." Visions of Miss Bennet swam before his eyes before he quickly blinked them away. "But when one wishes to speak of something of, uh, substance, then one naturally turns to one's gentlemen friends."

Bingley noticed that Darcy looked comfortable sitting there in his stocking feet, so he began tugging at his own boots. He pulled off the right one and tossed it carelessly aside, turning his attention to the other, tighter-fitting boot.

"When have you ever spoken to me about something of substance?" Darcy rolled his eyes and loosened his cravat.

"What? Have I not consulted you extensively on matters of…eh, ah, the stewardship of an estate? On gaining admittance to the finest of gentlemen's clubs? On the behaviour, comportment, and appearance of a gentleman? On the best way to shoot a pheasant or to train a hunting dog?" Bingley was panting, having finally achieved victory over the obdurate boot. He leaned back in his chair and reached for his glass.

Darcy gave a heavy sigh. "Yes, these are weighty matters, but there is something more, something alluring, even *passionate* about arguing with a woman about ideas. Yes, it is stimulating to have these discussions with one's equals over cigars and brandy, but with a woman—it is something else altogether."

"Is that so, Darcy? Truly, I do not see it."

"Oh, yes. The thrusting, the parrying, the tests of mental agility and strength—indeed, they take on a whole new meaning with a lady." Darcy poured himself a bit more brandy, sat back, and unbuttoned his waistcoat.

Bingley sat silently and pondered this for a few moments.

"Hmm. I had never thought of it in quite that way." He thought some more. "So what you are saying, my friend, is that arguing with a lady is merely a prelude to...you know." He waggled his eyebrows suggestively.

Darcy sighed, his brows raised in irritation. "No, not exactly."

"Do you mean you never noticed Miss Elizabeth's womanly charms or her fine eyes whilst 'sparring' with her?" Bingley grinned crookedly at the pinched look on Darcy's face. "I told you Caroline talked too much, did I not?"

Darcy pulled off his cravat. "Her eyes sparkled when she argued, Bingley." Had Darcy always had such a toothy smile?

"Oh! So do yours, Darcy. When you are talking to her, I mean." He flushed when he saw his friend's stricken expression and began mumbling about eyes, which was all he could think to talk about. "Caroline's eyes are always hard. Louisa's shoot this way and that; they make me dizzy. Miss Bennet's eyes were so blue, serene, and steady. But I saw no reciprocal affection." His eyes felt wet and he blinked rapidly. Where had that come from?

Looking alarmed, Darcy leaned forward. "All women are a mystery. It is our duty to delve, carve, and excavate our way through those layers—

"Aha! How surgical it all is! You say arguing is a prelude to discovering other charms. I knew it!" Bingley held out his near-empty glass and set it on the table next to Darcy's half-full one. "Darcy, have you felt it? Love? Have *you* admired a woman?"

Darcy shot unsteadily to his feet and strode to the fireplace. His knees appeared to tremble a bit as he walked in his stocking feet, and he laid a hand on the mantel as he caught his breath and regained his balance.

Bingley followed his lead and took a deep breath too. His fingers fumbled as he made to unbutton his constricting waistcoat. Zounds, brandy was quite filling! He felt that he was, at long last, on the verge of discovering something weighty and important about his friend. Darcy—the man who knew everything, who had travelled far and tasted well of the world—would reveal the secrets of a woman worth having! Surely, whatever sort of woman he admired would be the sort Bingley should admire as well. Darcy knew everything about everything, after all, and without a doubt, that must include women.

The great and all-knowing Darcy turned around. He looked…confused. This was odd. Darcy often looked angry or impatient or indulgent, but he never looked confused.

"Yes, Bingley. I believe I have. I have admired a lady."

"Zooks, man!" Bingley's head was swimming. So much knowledge. And so much brandy. He hoped Darcy would not bring up history or philosophy again. Or Greek. Please, not Greek. He thought he had better try to steer the conversation away from anything Greek and all other topics related to Macedonia, Troy, and the Bosphorus just to be on the safe side.

"I am all astonishment. You can banter with me and discuss business, and you may fence with your cousin. I cannot fence well, and as a military man, your cousin does not care to discuss estate business. But you have found a lady with whom you can banter, discuss estate concerns, *and* parry and thrust in other more rewarding ways?"

Bingley winked as well as one could after having guzzled three large tumblers of brandy and loudly whispered, "I mean in your bed, of course."

Darcy winced and nodded. "I took your meaning. Yes, these things would make a well-accomplished woman. In my eyes, at any rate."

Those eyes were quite bleary, Bingley observed blearily.

"And you are in love with a woman who meets such exacting requirements?" Even profoundly inebriated, Bingley found this rather surprising. Surely, his most accomplished friend had not been stung by love's arrow without breathing a word of it to him, his best friend.

Darcy shook his head and threw himself down into his chair. "Indeed, I am not. Parse my words, Bingley. I have met and admired her. It goes no further."

"But…"

Darcy reached into his pocket. His hand emerged clutching the handkerchief. And a ribbon. He stared at them for a moment. "As you see, I am still in an unmarried state. Perhaps I am too nice in my requirements." He returned the items to his pocket, picked up his glass, and drained the brandy within. He put the glass down on the tray, nudging it forward to indicate Bingley should refill it. Bingley was only too happy to oblige.

"Yes, there was a lady I admired once," Darcy confessed, "but she lacked a certain…social standing. I must uphold my responsibility to Pemberley and to my heritage. Admiration is not enough."

So said Darcy. It must be the truth. Bingley sighed. "Then what is enough? I did admire Jane's beauty, Darcy. We made a fine pair at dancing. And we both love puppies and ginger cake. But I never had a good argument with her. Not once. We were happy, you know, but I see now how dull it would have been with her. Especially compared to how you sparred with Miss Elizabeth."

Darcy's eyes widened. "Well, yes. She and I did have some memorable conversations." He briefly closed his eyes and cleared his throat. "But I spoke to your sisters as well, did I not?"

"Sisters are…they are an obstacle to love, Darcy. But not for you. Georgiana would never stop you from pursuing true love, would she?"

Why was Darcy biting his lip and looking sad? "Darcy! Did she stop you?"

His tall friend slid down deeply into his chair. "No, of course not. *I* stopped *myself* from endeavouring to discover whether she—the lady—was my true love. And now I shall never know."

Bingley's heart leapt. Darcy in unrequited love! He had suspected that Darcy's feelings had gone beyond mere admiration. Bingley had been in and out of love a hundred times, so he should know the signs. And now his friend, his *best* friend, needed his assistance. His! Bingley could not advise him on issues related to tenants nor on handling errant sisters, nor could he correct his fencing methods or discuss that dashed old Herodaquinas. But he could counsel him on matters of the heart! Hmm… Bingley stared at his toe; he should buy new stockings.

"Darcy, old man, I am pleased to hear you speak of true love. This is an area where I do have some experience. Perhaps I could help you discern whether the lady in question is indeed your true love." Bingley hiccuped and could not be bothered trying to hide it.

"Did we not just ascertain that you may be a master in the fine art of admiring women from afar but are a novice when it comes to truly understanding them?"

"Well, yes, but I am quite adept at admiring them. Is admiration not a short step from love?"

"I believe you have missed the point entirely," Darcy sputtered.

"No, I think not. Did your lady's eyes inspire you to write odes? Did her flawless, alabaster skin leave you desperate to see more?"

Darcy blushed. "Well, yes. Um, I... But—"

"There are no buts about it!" Bingley cried. *"A priori, cave canem:* it is true love."

"Bingley, I do not believe that means what you think it means—"

"Of course it does! Everyone knows that!" Bingley gestured wildly and clanked his glass against the decanter, knocking it over entirely and sending brandy trickling off the edge of the table and straight into Darcy's fine Hessian boots. "Damn."

Bingley dragged himself up to a standing position and leaned over the back of Darcy's chair to jerk the damask bell-pull, which fell to the ground with a ripping sound. "Damn. More brandy!" He dropped back down in his seat and threw a leg over the arm of the chair. His head was spinning oddly.

"No, no. Enough brandy. Bingley, you must listen to me on this. That is not true love. That is lust. True love is something else altogether: a meeting of minds, a sharing of...well...I could go on." Darcy paused and took a deep breath. His face was pale, his eyes piercing and bright.

Exhaling, he continued in a slow, deliberate and, to Bingley's ears, ever so slightly pompous voice. "But love without an equality of station, without a symmetry in circumstance, is doomed. It is irresponsible, especially on the side of the party with superiority of station. It will not do."

"Oh, hogwash!" Bingley turned completely sideways in his chair and laid his head on the table between them, leaving him to gaze upside down at

Darcy. Really, he had thought his friend was a bit…well, *deeper* than this. Even Bingley knew there was more to life than station and all that. He began to feel a bit light-headed with this discovery.

From this angle, Bingley could see certain things about Darcy's visage that had previously escaped his notice. The man had a small scar under his jaw. Perhaps from shaving or a boyhood fight? And was that a silver hair curling on his collar? Imagine that! He might have a cleft chin and be a superior physical specimen in every imaginable way, but he was, indeed, just a man like everyone else. Albeit one with a bruised heart, which made him worse off than Bingley. Ha! Darcy worse off than him! Truly? Hmm…

Darcy continued their earlier conversation, which Bingley now struggled to remember. Something about station or duty maybe, knowing Darcy. "It is not hogwash! I am surprised at you, Bingley, for thinking such nonsense, let alone saying it out loud. Have you not been listening to anything I have told you all these years?"

Dreamily and smiling a secret little smile, Bingley mumbled, "Love is not *everything*, Darcy, but surely it is *something*. Something wonderful."

With that, Bingley closed his eyes and gave a great snore that shook the glassware on the silver tray.

Darcy sat thinking about Bingley's words for a few minutes as he watched his friend's chest rise and fall.

"It may be something, my friend," he concluded sadly. "Something…but it is far from sufficient."

Just then, his man, Parsons, came into the room and looked at him enquiringly.

"Thank you, Parsons. There is a bit of a puddle on the carpet and some brandy in my boots. Please have Bingley conveyed to his usual room. I am for bed."

Darcy weaved slowly towards his rooms, grabbing now and again at the wall as he went, his head hanging down like a condemned man. When he arrived in his chambers, he pulled the handkerchief and hair ribbon from his pocket. Looking at them wistfully, he folded the handkerchief neatly into quarters and tucked the ribbon into it. He turned the beautifully embroidered initials over to hide them. Then he opened a drawer in the bureau near his bed and, reaching back as far as he could, regretfully, slowly, put the handkerchief underneath the small clothes therein. He closed the drawer firmly and walked away to gaze unseeing out the window. The snowflakes continued to swirl, catching the dim lamplight and illuminating, however briefly, the darkness of the night.

Part IV: In Vino Veritas

In Wine, There Is Truth

Darcy had sent word the previous week that he and his moustachioed cousin would be returning to London from Kent this evening, so Bingley clapped his fine new beaver hat on his head and set off in his carriage for Darcy's town house. His friend had been an absolute bear since that evening in January when they had drunk themselves into a stupor. Nothing was good enough! The ladies this season were shockingly lacking in beauty, accomplishment, and charm! This went on for weeks until even Bingley could not stand it any longer. He sincerely hoped that Darcy's time in Kent with his aunt and cousin might have removed that stick from his…oh, never mind.

As the carriage bounced along the foggy night-time streets, Bingley reflected that Darcy's bad mood had infected his own spirits as well. His natural insouciance, as dear Aunt Millie liked to call it, had been squashed down till he was almost as woeful as Darcy. Why, he had only eaten one ginger cake all day! This would not do. As much as Bingley admired his friend's handsome mien, quick mind, and warm companionship, he did not wish to be just like him in *that* particular way. He, Charles Horatio

49

Bingley, wished to smile and be happy. But he had not been able to enjoy himself lately. He had tried, really tried, to learn from Darcy and to find a lady with whom to spar. Surely, that would be as enjoyable as Darcy had said.

Just last week, he had attended a card party at Mrs. Johnson's home. There he noticed a pretty young lady, Miss Constance Weatherbee, who had fine, flashing eyes and seemed to be enjoying a lively conversation with several younger gentlemen in one corner. He recognised two of the young swains jostling for the lady's attention and felt he could comfortably join in their level of repartee. Sensing a need to act and not think too much on his approach, Bingley adjusted his cuffs and cut a straight path past the pretty girls in their spring dresses. Brantley and Smythe greeted him and made the proper introductions to Miss Weatherbee.

"Welcome to our little set, Mr. Bingley," she cooed. "We are in the middle of the most fascinating discussion about discourse, and how wars can begin and love affairs end based on simple misunderstandings of the language."

Bingley nodded eagerly. Yes, conversation was something about which he could…well, converse. "I see. Messages that go undelivered or are ill-read have changed the course of history."

Brantley coughed. "But when the tongue is involved, it is far worse."

Miss Weatherbee tittered, and the small group roared with laughter. This was great fun and just what Bingley had been seeking.

"Tongues do tangle," he offered. Yes, he was quite clever and could joust and parry.

"I have heard the tale of a man who set forth a sequence of events simply by misunderstanding the meaning of a simple phrase," Miss Weatherbee said.

The men leaned in, and she began her short tale about her brother's Cambridge classmate who had, while imbibing enthusiastically with his friends in the common rooms one evening, insisted that *ars gratia artis* did not mean "art is the reward of art," but "the donkey thanks the artist." Despite his friends' protests to the contrary, the classmate proclaimed loudly and repeatedly that this was undoubtedly what it meant. He was sure of it. The son of England's ambassador to Spain, himself quite inebriated, overheard this remark and thought it was such nonsense that it could only be secret code. He sent word of it to his father, who in turn sent it to the code breakers, and they determined it was valuable military intelligence that could help turn the tide in the Peninsula. Of course, it actually sent the troops off on a wild goose chase, waiting and waiting for a French battalion that never appeared. The English soldiers were so horribly drenched in the November rains that replacing their worsted uniforms required the early shearing of an entire generation of sheep, and the wool makers tripled their prices. Fortunes were made and lost as a result. It was a calamity on all counts. Such fools! What jingle-brains! Particularly the fellow who could not even translate the simplest of Latin sayings properly.

Good Lord—his infamous mistake! Bingley knew he was not good at Latin and never had been. Stunned, embarrassed, and desperately hopeful that no one there recognised him as the ill-informed idiot, a red-faced Bingley offered a weak rejoinder. "Perhaps he had wax in his ears. It can build up and impede proper understanding."

"Oh! How truly foul. I would hope not," replied a rather offended Miss Weatherbee. She turned away and whispered to Smythe, effectively dismissing Bingley. He found himself spending his evening playing whist with two spinsters and Mrs. Johnson's mute uncle. Such welcoming, unchallenging company came as a relief.

Yes, he was certainly trying to find this exemplary kind of lady, one to spar and joust with, just as Darcy had said. But secretly, he was beginning to believe that maybe he did not have what it took to do so. Indeed, the harder he tried, the more he found himself longing not for a lady who was adept at making a clever remark, inventing an amusing sally in Latin, or quoting an *a propos* poem, but for a lady who might be kind and gentle, who might see the best in everyone, who genuinely cared for the people around her. Someone like Jane Bennet, not to put too fine a point on it. But of course, *not* dear Jane, um, Miss Bennet, because after all, Darcy had rightly pointed out that she did not seem to care for him, not really. He wondered whether he would be able to find a lady with such qualities in the cut-throat sitting rooms of London. Still, he would keep trying. After all, Darcy was usually right about these things and nearly everything else. Yes, he was sure that Darcy would have a method for helping Bingley find a lovely lady who could spar with him a bit more…well, *gently*. It would be particularly nice if she liked puppies.

When he arrived at Darcy's town house, he found that the great man himself and his cousin were ensconced, as expected, in Darcy's study. Excitement at the thought of seeing Darcy—oh, and his jackanapes cousin too—after so long a separation swept all his concerns clean from his head. Enthusiastically thrusting his hat and coat at the butler—Jones, was it?—he bounded into the study. Well, this ought to be good! Surely, the colonel would have some ideas for a lively evening out on the town: A visit to a gaming hell, perhaps, or a race between man and beast? Had he read about such things, or had Hurst mentioned them?

Bingley entered the room with a great smile of anticipation, bellowing, "Darcy! You are back! Have I got some stories for you, old man! Colonel! What do you have in store for us this fine evening?"

Darcy waved his arm in Bingley's general direction, but did not greet him with his customary slap on the back. Bingley noticed that Darcy was, in fact, stalking about the room in his shirt and waistcoat, his cravat askew. It was most uncharacteristic of his usually fastidious friend and did not portend well for an evening out at the club or anywhere else for that matter.

"Evening, Bingley," said the colonel. He was as ruddy-faced as Bingley remembered. His moustache had grown to impressive proportions, and it quivered with indignation as he turned and spoke to Darcy.

"You ask that I shut it? You ask that I desist from pursuing this line of argument?" He shook his head with obvious disgust, and Bingley watched, fascinated, as the esteemed moustache drooped even further. "You are a proud fool, Darcy," the colonel thundered. "But you are a good man. Even a blind man can see that. But not a lady, apparently…"

What was this? Bingley gasped to himself. The colonel called Darcy a fool! And Darcy said nothing in defence? He observed his admirable friend assuming his usual position: face to the window, back to the room. Bingley noted something peculiar, however: Darcy's broad shoulders sagged, and his head hung down. What did they have here? Was there something about a lady? Then Darcy spoke:

"Archie, you are an ignoramus. The only things you understand are how to drink all of my best wine and brandy and how to remind me of my failings. I thank you." Darcy reached for the decanter and thrust it at his cousin's chest. "Make yourself useful. Fill it!" With this, he sat down hard in the chair next to his cousin.

Bingley laughed at Darcy's unexpected petulance. He usually was so steady and reasonable. "What the devil is wrong with you this evening, Darcy?"

"Nothing! Nothing is wrong with me. You know that seeing Lady Catherine always puts me in a foul temper." This was true. But normally, Darcy displayed that temper through making veiled, cutting remarks rather than by stomping around like a madman. Bingley found that he was both shocked and just the tiniest bit amused by his friend's tantrum. It seemed familiar, and he realised with some small sense of horror that Caroline often behaved in a similar fashion.

"Then I know just the thing to cheer you up, old man! We must go out for a night on the town. What tickles your fancy this evening? Dogs, cards, women?" He kept an eye on the colonel as he mentioned the latter. Women were really *his* province, after all.

Perhaps tonight, Darcy's worldly cousin would finally take them to one of those legendary houses of charming ladies about whom he was always rhapsodising. Perhaps if one of the ladies looked like Jane Bennet…

No! That was not what he wished. It would be wrong, so very wrong. A town miss would not have the fine inner qualities that truly made Jane… um, Miss Bennet, so lovely. On the other hand, Darcy, who was slouched in the chair with his arms crossed and his face vexed, looked to be in need of *some* kind of pampering and attention. However, it also appeared that if anyone attempted to touch him, he would tear that person's head off and devour it whole. Ah, *that* sort of jaunt would not do for him tonight either, then. The man needed companionship—brotherly companionship—the kind only his cousin and Bingley could provide.

But Darcy was mumbling to himself about whatever it was they had been discussing ages ago. Why could the fellow not keep up? What did he mean by "last man in the world"? Bingley took it upon himself to make enquiries.

"Darcy," he said kindly, "I believe you need a bit of cheering up."

"Playing some stupid game of chance will not lift my spirits. You know I abhor that sort of thing—the insipid conversation, the low company…"

"The theatre, then? That would be capital!" Bingley loved the theatre, especially the comedies. He knew Darcy would not approve of strongmen, magic tricks, acrobats, or dancing bears—the sorts of things that Bingley secretly adored. But no doubt Shakespeare or some other high-minded-but-humorous chap might be just the thing?

"Surely not!" Darcy's face was as dark as a thundercloud. "Absolutely not. I am in no mood for comedy—to say nothing at all of tragedy! My God, man."

Clearly, this called for a more grandiose gesture of some sort since Darcy had even rejected his beloved Shakespeare. Well, Bingley knew just the thing. "Darcy, prepare yourself for the evening of a lifetime! Unlock your liquor cabinets and fill the decanters with your finest spirits. I challenge you at billiards! You provide the brandy, and I shall provide you a contest for the ages."

The colonel rolled his eyes. "You are hitting my poor cousin in one of his endless sore spots, Bingley: his precious French brandy." He broke into a grin, and his enormous furry lips stretched wide. "Come on then! To the billiards room."

Bingley eagerly grabbed several glasses and made to follow the colonel, but Darcy did not move a muscle.

The colonel looked at him with a gimlet eye, and in his most commanding voice, barked, "Darcy! Up! No more complaints and no more self-pity! Transport your sorry self to the billiards room *immediately*!"

In spite of his sorry self, Darcy flashed the tiniest hint of a smile. "And just who do you think you are to order me around in this absurd fashion?"

The colonel grinned. "Disregard my many decorations and medals as you will. I certainly have more experience than you do in healing wounds such as those you have just suffered."

A wound? Had Darcy been thrown from a horse? Had a fencing accident? Got the French disease? My God!

The colonel herded Darcy and a worried Bingley down the hall to the billiards room. Bingley put the drinking glasses on a side table by the window seat.

"Let us go to it. Jackets off and at the ready," snapped the colonel with military precision as he and Bingley launched their coats towards a chair by the wall.

He peered at the decanter he had carried in from the study and then glanced at Darcy. "Already stripped down, are we? You and Bingley are up first. Let us have short games, fifteen minutes per game, in pairs, double elimination. And with every point lost, a great swig of brandy!" He lifted the decanter in the air.

Darcy looked at him sourly. "Your primary objective is thus clearly revealed."

The colonel laughed. "Aha, you have seen right through me! What is the nature of your objection? Do you require stakes other than the pleasure of seeing your companions fall down drunk? Or perhaps you wish to drink yourself into a stupor but fear you will not be forced to drink because you are such a superior player?"

This provoked chuckles from the three men because they, in fact, were rather evenly matched. Darcy was an excellent, versatile player, the colonel had a powerful arm, and Bingley was, unaccountably, rather a genius with the geometry and physics of a difficult shot.

"Yes, I see we shall have to sweeten the pot with a wager!" exclaimed Bingley. This would be just the thing to distract Darcy. "If I win, Darcy must tell me the story of his wound. If I lose, I shall tell you about a great discovery of mine."

His two friends exchanged bemused glances. "And what is at stake for me?"

asked the colonel, putting down the decanter and picking up a cue stick. "I only win the tale of Darcy's woe or the great Bingley disclosure? One I have already heard, and the other would try my patience." He pointed his stick at a painting of a fox hunt. "You two can talk to each other until you turn blue, but I choose a hunt with you as my grousing side men for my reward."

Bingley laughed, Darcy scowled, and the game was on. Every point scored—every ball pocketed, every red ball struck—required another great slurp of brandy, and thus each man's forward progress seemed to lessen Bingley's hope for victory and increased the quivering in his legs and arms. The match was closely fought to the end, and by the time Bingley emerged victorious with fifty points to Darcy's forty-eight, he had to hang onto the side of the billiards table to keep his balance.

Upon his defeat, Darcy immediately gave up trying to remain upright and sprawled with a resounding thud on the cushioned window seat. From there, he viewed the unfolding contest between Bingley and the colonel.

"Are you sure you wish to continue playing, Bingley?" asked the colonel with some solicitude, taking a long drink of brandy and wiping his moustache on his sleeve with a flourish. "It hardly seems fair. Fat lot of good your geometry prowess will do you now."

"Ah, but you know how much he hates a hunt, Archie," Darcy threw in. "He would do anything to avoid that."

"Nonsense! I shall be all right," Bingley said brightly, though privately he wondered whether he would be able to stand much longer. "Colonel, if you please, oblige me by drinking a glass or two more, and then we shall call it even."

The colonel did oblige, and the game commenced. He won the right to break and immediately scored three points, forcing Bingley to drink. Damn. A few more shots back and forth, a few more drinks, and the colonel had backed Bingley into an impossible shot, the red balls blocked by the colonel's cue ball. Bingley staggered back and forth along the table, looking for the right angle. He found what looked to be a way around the problem, and leant over to get a good look down the cue stick, protractor angles and force vectors swimming before his eyes. Dash it all, why were there two red balls and four white ones on the table instead of the usual one and two? And which one amongst all those balls was he supposed to hit? It was probably not a good idea to ask one of his companions, so he would just do his best. He lined up the balls, pulled back his cue, and swung his arm forward as hard as he could.

But he must have miscalculated because, rather than the clicking and thudding of ivory balls, the sound of tearing fabric filled the air. Oh dear. His cue stick had ripped a great gash across the felt, slicing the table top from stem to stern like a ghastly war wound. At least there was no blood, but glimpses of slate beneath the shredded felt peeped out like bone from the enormous rent. Darcy closed his eyes in what Bingley could only assume was pain.

The colonel laughed as though he had never seen anything so funny. He walked around the table to throw his arm over Bingley's shoulders and roared, "I must say, old man, that we are through with billiards for the evening." With his ear ringing and his head spinning, Bingley shut his eyes and felt the colonel guide him over to a chair near Darcy's window seat. At least he would not have to hunt. He really did hate hunting, chasing after that poor, adorable little fox and rejoicing over the limp bodies of birds and hares…

Opening his eyes and glancing over at the grisly sight of the torn and scarred billiard table, Bingley was flooded with terrible shame as well as some pain on his friend's behalf. Another wound for poor ol' Darce. Perhaps a bit more brandy would soothe everyone's nerves. He fumbled for the decanter on the table next to him and reached over to refill Darcy's glass before holding the brandy aloft like some great prize and offering it to the colonel. That man took it from his fist and filled Bingley's glass before retreating to the scene of the devastation, perching cross-legged on the edge of the table, carafe in hand. It looked as though, if he crossed his arms and dipped his head like a genie, the colonel might float off altogether, riding the table like a magic carpet. That would be more exciting than those cavalry charges he was always leading. Perhaps Bingley could ride with him on the carpet.

"Colonel—"

"Archie. For God's sake, call me Archie. How many times do I have to tell you?" The colonel gave him a fierce look.

Bingley found that he just could not say it. "Hmm…Colonel, I wonder how many passengers can fit on a magic carpet?"

He paused, glancing between the two cousins and wondering at the odd looks they were exchanging. Darcy coughed lightly and began tugging at his boots.

"Well, Bingley, it depends on what one is flying with as cargo." The colonel chuckled. "Brandy and magic lanterns or muskets and May flowers. Is there a thought you wish to share?"

"Well, yes, there is." Bingley watched Darcy pull off his Hessians. Such fine leathers the man had in his closet. He should ask whether he might visit Darcy's shoemaker. They could go together.

"Darcy, whilst you were away, I did my best to find myself an accomplished woman, just as you said," Bingley babbled. "But I failed. I fear I must be doing something wrong, my friend."

The colonel must have inadvertently inhaled most of his mouthful of brandy when he began to guffaw loudly at this last remark. Really, Bingley could not understand what was so amusing about his lacklustre love life. Once the colonel had ceased coughing and caught his breath, he said, "Truly? Darcy is giving you advice about women? How rich!" And he laughed some more. Darcy gave him the evil eye but did not say a word to rebut his statement.

Bingley felt even more bewildered. "Why do you say that, old man? Darcy has impeccable judgment in all things."

Again, the colonel snickered. "It seems he knows nothing of women. You must pay no heed to any advice he has ever given you on this subject. And I would strongly suggest you reconsider any counsel he may have given you on other subjects as well."

"Why would you joke about such a thing?" Bingley felt obliged to defend his friend from the colonel's barbs although he *had* himself begun to wonder.

"Bingley, do not trouble yourself," Darcy said slowly. "My cousin is quite right. Please forget all that I said to you before."

"But why?" Bingley's head was spinning. "Give me one good reason."

"Darcy has recently been shown quite forcefully that his judgment with regard to women is flawed indeed. He suffered quite a setdown, in fact."

A lady? What *lady* would give Darcy a setdown? The only lady Bingley could think of whom Darcy might have encountered in Kent, one capable of giving him a setdown of any kind, was his aunt. What was her name again? He knew that, earlier in the evening, Darcy had said her name, but it slipped his mind just now. Something beginning with a C. Lady Cecilia? Lady Celeste? Bingley could not for the life of him remember.

Trying to manoeuvre his way through his confusion, he enquired, "I am afraid I do not quite follow you. In what way were you mistaken about your aunt, Lady Kuh-hrrrrmph?" He cleared his throat and smiled pleasantly.

Darcy eyed him, perplexed. "My *aunt*?" The colonel laughed again, and Darcy shot him a look that could have killed a horse at twenty paces. The colonel clamped his lips together and his ruddy cheeks shaded into a sort of burgundy colour, or perhaps it was Bordeaux.

"Yes, the lady in Kent," Bingley muttered. Apparently, he had something wrong, but he could not put his finger on just what. Confused as he was about a lady offending Darcy, he was deeply relieved that his best friend had not suffered fencing wounds or the raging boils said to spread from the dreaded French disease.

"No, no, not our aunt, though she had a few choice words for both of us as usual," replied the colonel, refilling their brandy glasses with a practised flip of the wrist. "No, Darcy received a reprimand from an entirely different feminine source."

Then Bingley remembered the cousin. What was her name? He thought it began with an H. Or a D. Oh, if only he were better with names.

Antigone! By Jove, that was it! Cousin Antigone. He was sure of it. Bingley struggled to remember the story that Darcy had recounted once when they were out for a ride. Bingley had tried hard to pay attention, but there had been some particularly beautiful and distracting wild flowers in bloom that day. Ah, it was beginning to come back to him now. There were expectations that Darcy would marry Cousin Antigone, yes, yes. He must have proposed to her, which was peculiar since Darcy had hinted he wanted nothing to do with her. And she had given him a setdown? Not accepted him? That seemed strange. Bingley recalled hearing she was a sickly, mousy girl.

"She turned you down? Incredible!" Bingley cried, his voice loud and animated. "That hardly seems in character. I thought you said she was *hoping* for your addresses! *Expecting* them, even! But were you not dead set against it? Why on earth did you propose to her?"

"Why indeed?" The colonel smirked.

"No wonder you are in such a foul temper." Bingley spoke over Darcy, who was trying without success to get a word in edgewise. "Imagine! Imagine any woman saying no to such a splendid match! Let alone *her.*" He noticed Darcy's face flushing bright red. He must have hit the nail on the head. Capital!

How could this cousin of his have done such a thing? Was she like Miss Elizabeth Bennet, heedless of the charms of his good friend and his cleft chin? Miss Antigone knew him at least as well as anyone did. In a sitting room sort of way. And had they not romped as children? Played games with the little colonel? Bingley wondered whether the colonel had had such a magnificent moustache when he was a young boy. Likely not. Oh, but the girl cousin…Antigone. No! It was *Anne*, of course, not Antigone! What a silly mistake! Antigone was that Norse goddess Darcy liked to go on and on about. Anne De Bourgh was infirm or something, was she not? He could not recall the problem exactly. Was she feeble-minded, or was she merely knock-kneed and consumptive?

Damn. Darcy had likely asked her to dance a reel too, and her sickly constitution had revolted at the thought of touching his firm hands. What was it the colonel—Archie, as that man was constantly urging Bingley to call him—had said about Anne? Ah, yes; in looks, she favoured an ostrich who had gone hungry for too long and then swallowed an especially unpleasant leaf.

When had the man seen an ostrich? He had never been to Africa as far as Bingley knew. But then one could never tell with military men. Bingley himself had only glimpsed an ostrich in one of Darcy's thick books, the animal encyclopaedia with etchings, drawings, and flighty imaginings. It was his favourite. No Greek in that tome—just some Latin he could disregard because the pictures told the real story.

"Bingley...Bingley!" Bingley looked up, caught out in his musings.

"If you wish to stay this evening, I have two requests for you: do not listen to anything my cousin tells you, and set aside any angry words you hear from me." Darcy sighed. "It has been a trying few days." He sank down deeper into the window seat.

Bingley studied his friend. He did look worn down, even taking into account the large volume of brandy he had recently consumed. His face was pale and rather smudged under the eyes, which lacked their customary clarity, seemed smaller than usual, and looked rather bloodshot. Dare Bingley ask about these trying few days? Or should he take the lead in changing the course of conversation and ask about, say, something learned? About philosophy...or cheese...or perhaps sundials? Or those newfangled, floating inventions, hot air balloons?

Hot air balloons. Lovely things. He had seen them once or twice but never had the nerve to ride in one. He imagined that the colonel probably had, even if he had never been to Africa. Bingley wondered how the colonel's parents felt about all his hot air balloon rides and other dangerous, swashbuckling adventures. Were they proud of him or frightened and worried? Or maybe they took it as a matter of course since he was the madcap second son. Or perhaps they were wrapped up in their own affairs and paid him no attention at all. Maybe they fought constantly. Oh dear. How sad.

"Are your parents a happy pair, Colonel...um, Archie? Colonel Archie?"

The colonel jerked his head up a bit, perhaps in surprise at this new topic of conversation or by Bingley's use of his Christian name. Bingley hoped his question had not been too impertinent. Perhaps not, because now the moustachioed one exchanged a bemused glance with his cousin. "Ah, my father is the brother of Lady Catherine in every way one can imagine. My mother, on the other hand, is a lovely practitioner of amiability and accommodation."

Good. It seemed they did not argue all the time after all. "You are fortunate to have them both still on this earth." Bingley tried hard to suppress the tinge of sadness and envy he heard in his own quiet voice. He felt a tightness in his chest. It might actually have been his stomach, however, which was full only of brandy and a biscuit or two that he had eaten in his study earlier in the evening whilst hiding from Caroline and her latest malicious tale of the *ton*. Oh, she was dreadful. She always had been.

"My parents adored each other, or so I have been told," Darcy said wistfully. "I do not remember seeing them sharing time together often, but I was a mere boy. They appeared content. They were happy when Georgiana was born. I want to think that they were always so." He sighed and slouched down into the window seat, turning his head towards the wall. "A love match—that is what a marriage should be."

What was that? Had Fitzwilliam Tiberius Darcy just said that marriage should be a love match? What about all that earlier talk about equality of station and doom-filled symmetry? Bingley opened his mouth to protest the odd circumstance of Darcy's indecisiveness, but he heard a peculiar sound. His head swivelled. From his perch on the table, the colonel had sighed. Bingley glanced over and found him looking thoughtfully at Darcy. His eyes betrayed an unexpected sadness, and seeing the gruff man softening wrenched something loose inside him.

"My parents were a happy pair," Bingley said, just above a whisper. "As I recall, my mother was all that was gentle and kind, and my father would sing to her. Losing them both at once was horrible." He tearfully recounted the story of his parents' deaths. Darcy knew it well, of course.

Archie's eyes widened as the sad tale unfolded, and he looked to his cousin apprehensively at Bingley's unexpected display of emotion.

Darcy—stretched out on the window seat, his stocking feet up on the wall—had been preoccupied with drawing hearts and arrows on the glass. Now he turned and watched his friend. "It was tragic, Bingley," he said gently, "but the smoke was thick, and they did not suffer. And they were together."

"Bound in life and death," Bingley murmured.

"Bound by love," whispered Darcy.

There was a long silence in the room, broken only by the sounds of their breathing and the low rumble of an empty stomach or two.

In the quiet, the customary cacophony inside Bingley's head subsided rather more than usual. One bright, clear thought remained, and Bingley suddenly felt possessed of a powerful need to tell his friend something that had been percolating in the back of his mind for some time now, his conviction about it growing nearly unnoticed as time passed. He was not obliged to share it, he knew, since he had not precisely lost the wager at billiards, but he felt *moved* to do so. "Darcy, I have come to a conclusion. An important conclusion, you know."

"What is that, Bingley?"

"I was truly in love with Jane Bennet."

Darcy repositioned his legs higher on the wall and waved the hand not clutching his brandy glass. "You admired her excessively, but as I think we established—"

"No. *No.* I did admire her beauty, yes. But it was more than that. I was a better man when I was with her."

The colonel looked at him with open curiosity. "What do you mean, Bingley?"

"I was more steady to my purpose. She gently and kindly nudged me along and kept my train of thought from…" He groped for just the right word, but it eluded his grasp.

Darcy sat up and rose unsteadily to his feet. He and Archie waited in silence until the latter could stand it no longer and broke in. "Wandering?"

Bingley nodded vigorously and wished he had not. "Yes, just so. I was truly in love with her as I had never been before. I only admired all those other ladies, as you said. If only she had felt the same about me… Thank you, Darcy, for keeping me from losing myself wholly to her when she did not love me in return."

Darcy turned away quickly but not before Bingley noticed that his face was fiercely red, his handsome features contorted with emotion. He could swear it was something like embarrassment or remorse. This was an unusual sight to behold, and he could not understand what might have inspired such feelings in his friend. Such an estimable, honest, honourable man surely would have no cause for them. Perhaps Bingley had misinterpreted his expression, or Darcy was simply flushed with modesty, though that did not seem likely. Darcy moved to say something, still turned away so as not to meet Bingley's eye, but Bingley stood and cleared his throat, preventing Darcy from speaking.

Bingley spoke thickly, his head swimming with emotion and brandy, but he expressed himself with great passion. "Darcy, you stopped me before I could hand my heart to a lady who held no regard for me. That is true friendship. I am grateful, my friend. My wonderful friend."

Darcy sensed Bingley behind him then felt the shorter man's arms wrap around his shoulders in an awkward hug. He froze and averted his eyes from his cousin's laughing visage.

"Thank you, Dar…"

Darcy stumbled forward with the full weight of a drunk, sleeping Bingley on his back. Twisting around and pulling at Bingley's hands, Darcy clumsily deposited him onto the window seat before lifting his feet and stretching him out onto the long bench.

"*Absentem laedit cum ebrio qui litigat,*" mumbled Darcy. He glanced at his cousin, never a student of Latin, and translated. "To quarrel with a drunk is to wrong a man who is not even there."

Archie rolled his eyes before he looked at Darcy with obvious pity. "Well, Cousin, that was quite a great confession Bingley made there. You will have to tell him some time."

"Yes. I…I cannot bear to do it this evening." Darcy leaned against the wall with one hand, his head down in defeat, and gazed upon his sleeping friend.

The colonel jumped down from his perch and clapped him on the back.

"No, I think you have suffered enough humiliation for the next fortnight or so. Save it till later. Just imagine how exponentially his anger will have grown by the time all is revealed!"

Darcy flinched and took a few unsteady steps towards the near empty decanter.

"Will you confess all to him or only the parts that affect his heart? Does he have any idea what you have been grappling with all these many months?" Archie rubbed his stomach and gazed at his cousin. "You would feel far better if you ate something."

Darcy shook his head, then immediately stopped and winced from the pain. "Archie, do you not understand? I do not wish to feel anything. I want to stop thinking and remembering and castigating myself." He poured the last of the golden liquid into his glass and stared at it. In a low voice, he asked, "Is there not such a thing as true love? Is it possible for it to be felt only on one side?" He sighed deeply. "Which circle of hell is this?"

Bingley began snoring and curled up into a tight ball. The colonel covered him with his discarded jacket and belched.

"Love's true arrow can never go awry, Darcy. The archer must practice, but he gains proficiency and, in the end, wins the heart he seeks. Or finds a new target."

Confused, Darcy rubbed his neck. "I have never asked, Archie. Do you speak of yourself? Have *you* been wounded by Cupid's arrow?"

The colonel smirked and turned away. "Not as you have been. I have never been that clumsy with a declaration." He snatched a cushion from the settee and restored himself to his perch atop the ruined billiards table. He stretched out, boots crossed at the ankles, laid his head on the purloined pad, and groaned. "There was a blonde girl in Rouen who once caught my eye and nearly captured my heart."

Darcy sat with a thud upon the settee. "But when? I never knew."

"We all have our secrets, Darcy. Yours are kept from Bingley but given to me."

"And yours?"

"Mine go with me to the grave, for better or for worse."

Darcy grumbled, "Damn you. You know of my humiliation, of my heartbreak. You were there—nay, responsible—for my introduction to the fair sex and to the havoc wreaked by brandy and wine. You have seen me at my worst as I am now, hopeless and grim. But all I can offer you is a chamber safe from your parents' meddling?"

The colonel shook his head. "Darcy, I like your friend. He makes me laugh. But you are not my Bingley; you offer me so much more as a cousin, friend, and confidant. I simply do not have much to tell. I..." He hesitated and swallowed the last of his brandy. "I have not felt as you feel; I have not loved. I do not know whether I have that capacity."

"I believe you do, Archie. You have an enormous heart. But I wonder, nevertheless, whether you have the right of it, protecting yourself as you do. Perhaps I should learn from your example. Love may not be worth the risk. Nor the pain."

"Perhaps. See if you still cling to this foolish notion in the light of day. But for now, let us ring for Parsons to tend to Bingley and follow his example by setting off for the Land of Nod."

Darcy assented and tugged on the bell pull. The two men staggered towards the door, the colonel holding up his taller cousin as they made their way from the room. Neither of them noticed that Bingley, still on the bench and with one bleary but speculative eye open, watched them leave.

Part V: Amantes Sunt Amentes
Lovers Are Lunatics

Caroline and Louisa had been completely unbearable all afternoon, and Darcy was at least somewhat to blame. He had left the rest of the travelling party that morning at the inn where they had spent the night, and he had ridden ahead to Pemberley to take care of some estate business. Or so he said. Bingley wondered whether his great friend simply had had enough of listening to the Bickering Bingley Sisters. With great envy, Bingley had watched him gallop off as the sisters criticised, gossiped, and preened with increasing energy the farther away Darcy's figure retreated. The carriage became hotter and the air closer with each of their vile words.

Eventually, poor Georgiana pleaded a headache and retreated to the other carriage with her companion, leaving Bingley to face his sisters alone. Oh, and Hurst, sawing logs in the corner. It hardly seemed fair that Darcy had escaped all this. But since Bingley's family were to be guests of the Darcys, and poor Darcy would be fighting off Caroline's hints, swoons, and fawning for the next fortnight, he could hardly begrudge his friend a few hours of peace and quiet. But he did, a bit, just to himself.

Finally, though, after one too many stories about how *low and unfashionable*

Caroline found one of her *best and dearest* friends, Bingley was rather shocked to discover that he, too, had had enough. That rarely happened, so he decided to ride ahead as well. If he had to spend one more moment listening to Caroline and Louisa criticise all the ladies in London, he might just burst into some sort of fiery conflagration. Well, he probably would not, not really. The thought of spontaneously combusting inside the carriage struck him as being rather amusing actually. What looks of horror would his sisters wear as they watched him go up in flames? Hurst probably would not move at all since he seemed to be comatose, but maybe the noise and smoke would wake him. Still, that was best avoided. It was Darcy's carriage, after all.

So when they changed horses after the midday meal, he left the carriage and rode off towards Pemberley. Bingley was not proud of this decision. In fact, he felt terrible leaving Georgiana to them, but it could not be helped. It was worrisome, however, that Darcy might not be so forgiving of Bingley's leaving Georgiana behind as a sacrificial lamb. He would have to concoct a reasonable explanation for his actions and hope that she would arrive unscathed. The party was due at Pemberley by mid-morning the next day, so she would have to fend for herself until then. When he enquired, as any polite gentleman would do, Georgiana insisted she did not mind; she planned to tell Caroline and the Hursts that she continued to feel ill and wished to rest in the second carriage for the duration of the trip. But that would still leave her in their company at the inn during supper and a dreadful evening in a sitting room. But it was too late for regrets; the die was cast.

Daylight was just beginning to fade as Bingley rode up the long, sweeping drive to Pemberley's great house. Darkness came late in the North. Bingley's stomach growled, and his mouth watered in anticipation of the tasty treats that Mrs. Reynolds doubtless had at the ready.

After leaving his horse at the stable, Bingley bounded into the house and received word from a footman that Darcy was in his study. When Bingley found him there, Darcy was pacing around as if in a trance. He was an odd sight to behold. His clothing was hanging rather haphazardly from his body, and his hair was positively standing on end. Most peculiar of all, it appeared he was slightly damp. Or, more precisely, that he had once been damp and now had dried in a most crumpled and bedraggled manner. And his noble face held such a strange and hopeful expression that Bingley nearly burst with amused curiosity.

"Bingley! What a wonderful surprise! I was not expecting you until tomorrow morning!" This was interesting since Darcy usually greeted him with warmth but not with this sort of enthusiasm.

His friend's happiness immediately lifted his own mood, and Bingley clapped him on the shoulder. "Darcy! What has you so jolly, old friend? You are positively glowing! Have you got into the brandy again? It is not yet dark outside!"

Darcy flushed to the tips of his ears. "What? No, no, nothing like that. Simply glad to be home, that is all." Bingley was not completely sure of it since he was no expert at reading others' expressions, but it seemed to him that Darcy was…well, lying…not to put too fine a point on it.

Bingley considered this for a moment just to make certain. No, it could not be. Bingley realised he had never, not even once, caught Darcy in anything remotely close to a fib, a white lie, or any sort of falsehood. True, his friend was often selective in the facts he shared, but certainly, he would not tell a barefaced lie about something that had him positively humming with enthusiasm. Well, Bingley would be patient, and all would be revealed.

He was now overjoyed that he had ridden ahead in spite of his earlier feelings of guilt over leaving Georgiana. He would have all evening and even the early morning hours to squeeze, wring, or wrestle the truth from his friend before they were interrupted by the others. Things could only turn sour once his sisters arrived. Best to work his wiles now to shore up Darcy's happy foundation. My God, he was smiling. No—beaming! It was that toothy grin he had seen last January and not once since, not even when they had their billiards night with old Archie. The cleft in Darcy's chin disappeared when he smiled? Interesting. Now you see it; now you don't.

Darcy cleared his throat and spoke with what seemed to Bingley to be feigned nonchalance. "Bingley, I hesitate to bring this up for reasons that will become evident, but the most peculiar thing happened this afternoon. I am sure you will never guess who was here when I arrived."

Bingley tried to think of the least likely person Darcy might have encountered upon his arrival at Pemberley. "Napoleon Bonaparte? Beau Brummell? Um…Cicero?" Knowing Darcy, this had to involve Latin and some damn Roman.

"Do not be absurd, Bingley. You know very well that Cicero is dead. Still, you truly will never guess, so I shall have to tell you: Miss Elizabeth Bennet and her aunt and uncle, Mr. and Mrs. Gardiner." Darcy bit his bottom lip and nodded. "The ones from Cheapside."

Bingley was stunned. How many times since the twenty-sixth of November had he thought of Miss Jane Bennet? At first, he had tried to deny that he ever had any real feelings for her, and he had let his admiration for Darcy and his desire to be more like his friend overrule his own good sense. Not that he really had good sense about anything. He was far more likely to trust the judgment of others than to rely on his own poor powers of discernment. But still, he had been right to listen to Darcy with regard to dear Jane. There was no doubt about it, none at all. Nevertheless, thinking about her always left him feeling full of melancholy and regret—a most unusual and uncomfortable sensation as he was used to happily gliding through life. For the most part, he had been untouched by the dramas, tragedies, and tensions that made up other people's lives. It made Caroline angry. She always had such purpose in her words and in her stride, yet she had to depend on him—the man of the family—to lead their way in the world. It had hardened her eyes.

But why was he thinking about Caroline when Darcy was talking about the Bennets? Here was a chance to hear more about dear Jane from her sister. Suddenly, he was so eager that he could hardly bear it. "Miss Elizabeth Bennet is here?" Oh, it felt so wonderful to say "Bennet" out loud instead of just mouthing the word (with Jane's name appended to it) in front of the mirror.

"Not *here*. Not here *now*. She was here earlier, visiting the park."

Oh. Bingley was crestfallen. Here and gone and without her sister. Why had she been here? Had she left word for him, for the dolt who did not understand love or recognise her sister's worth or grasp how to parry and thrust? Verbally, anyway?

"But why here?"

Darcy's face turned a deep crimson. "They were on holiday, um, *are* on holiday and touring the area. Miss Elizabeth's aunt is from Lambton. You know, the village just outside Pemberley. They are here for a visit."

Bingley stared at his friend, astonished at the wealth of information he had gleaned. "You spent some time with them?"

"No, no, no," Darcy replied quickly, shaking his head. "Well, yes. Some. Bingley, excuse me. You have come all this way, you are still in your travelling clothes, and I have yet to offer you a drink. Please, sit down." He gestured to one of the leather wing chairs he favoured. All his homes were littered with them. "May I order you some tea or perhaps some—?"

"Brandy. I would like a brandy."

"Brandy?" Darcy enquired, his brow furrowed. "Surely, you must have something to eat first. Would brandy agree with you after that long ride in the hot sun?"

Ah, Darcy was worried about his boots or his rugs or his billiard table. Fair enough, though Bingley wished to protest that he had always been able to hold his liquor—unlike some men he could name. Still, he would *indeed* like some brandy, especially considering how concerned he was that Darcy might at any time ask where Georgiana was. What on earth would he say? He needed a quick excuse! Maybe he could distract his friend by talking about something else. What was it that Darcy had told him? Oh, yes! How could he have forgotten? Miss Elizabeth!

"Yes, Darcy, brandy. It has been a long day, and you have a story to tell. I must know everything about Miss Elizabeth's visit. I should like to have seen her."

Darcy handed his friend a glass of brandy and picked up his cup of tea. "Shall I have some food sent in?"

"Oh yes, please. What do you have on hand? Do you suppose the kitchen has a duck pasty or two? Perhaps some sausages or a partridge? Oh, or Cook's lovely creamed potatoes… And what about some of those delicious sticky buns or her famous berry tarts?" Bingley realised that this might be a bit too much to ask, but he was ravenously hungry.

Well acquainted with Bingley's enormous appetite, Darcy merely nodded and rang for Mrs. Reynolds. "Yes, excellent idea."

"Oh, that reminds me, what is the damage to your billiards table?" Bingley flushed, thinking about the table he had left in ruins earlier in the spring. He cleared his throat. "Well, I know what the *damage* was. What I mean is: How much do I owe you for its repair?"

"Nonsense. You owe me nothing. We had quite a bit to drink that evening, and if you had not done the honours, then Archie or I would have done so sooner or later. Damn soldiers' drinking games."

Bingley shook his head in disbelief. He could not imagine his talented friend eviscerating a billiards table. Not unintentionally anyway. "No, never. Please let me take care of it, old chap."

"No, no. Truly, never mind. All in a good night's fun."

That *had* been an interesting evening, Bingley reflected with some wistfulness. Not that he remembered it too clearly. He recalled something about the colonel…um, Archie flying around on a magic carpet. That could not really have happened, of course. Could it? No, no, that must have been the brandy talking. Something about a hot air balloon as well, and that seemed a bit more likely, although it still seemed improbable that they had actually taken flight in Darcy's town house. Also something about an ostrich… In any case, the material point was that *something* had happened after the hot air balloon episode, and that *something* was the conversation he vaguely remembered overhearing between Darcy and the colonel. Archie. Perhaps he had dreamed it along with the colonel's magic carpet, but he thought not.

It seemed to have been a weighty and important conversation, but Bingley could not quite recall the subject. Something Darcy was not telling him? Something to do with a woman? Darcy had never explained what had happened with his cousin Anne in Kent. And, come to think of it, he had never confirmed that it actually had been Anne at all. Perhaps it was some other lady who had turned Darcy down. Imagine that! If only he could reach through that evening's brandy-induced haze to retrieve the memory of exactly what the two cousins had been talking about.

Bingley's train of thought was interrupted by Mrs. Reynolds's entrance into the study. After a proper greeting was exchanged, Bingley enquired about the availability of his dreamed-for meal and was delighted to discover that nearly all of it was already waiting in the kitchen. He was Mrs. R's favourite *bon vivant*, and she was well acquainted with his culinary tastes. She clucked and fussed a bit because the berry tarts would not be ready till the next day—when she had expected him to arrive. Bingley suddenly realised that Mrs. R might be curious about Georgiana's whereabouts, and he was sorely relieved when she bustled out of the room without enquiring after the girl.

After her departure, the friends settled into their chairs by the window. Darcy's knee was bouncing up and down, Bingley noted with surprise. How annoying. No wonder his sisters, his aunts, and Darcy himself constantly chastised Bingley about his own free-spirited limbs.

Limbs. He remembered Darcy's limbs, his legs in particular, stretched high up on the wall that evening, the evening of the billiards contest for the ages. He had looked so relaxed then, even elegant in his drunken melancholy, whilst he was agitated now. Rather as he had been back on that long, cold night in January when they had discussed his verbal parries with Miss Elizabeth. What had that been about, anyway?

"Darcy, tell me about Miss Elizabeth's visit. Did you know she would be at Pemberley? Was it a surprise or a planned rendezvous?" He waggled his eyebrows to emphasise his clever joke.

"For God's sake, Bingley. What do you imply? Miss Elizabeth and I are merely acquaintances in a tenuous sort of manner. She is travelling with her aunt and uncle, they stopped here and walked the gardens, and they encountered me only because I arrived a day earlier than expected. In fact, they believed that none of the family were here." Darcy glared at Bingley, his face flushed and eyes bright. He clanked his teacup down on the saucer with no little discomposure and poured a bit of brandy into a nearby glass. He eyed it then took a deep swallow.

"In what manner did you encounter her? Them?"

"Oh. I rode in, felt a bit overheated in the sun, and stopped by the pond. Aeschylus needed a drink."

The Greek steed. That fine piece of horseflesh had a sweet disposition and a white heart-shaped dot on the tip of his nose, and Darcy had named him after a poet instead of something truly memorable such as Avenger, Sport, or Thunder. The man was hopeless.

"Did your horse push you into the pond? Is that why you are still a bit damp?"

Darcy froze.

"Good God, Darcy! Did Miss Elizabeth see you this way, soaked and dishevelled?"

"Of course not. I had changed my clothing." Darcy abruptly stood and walked across the room to an ornate mirror. He grimaced at his reflection and began smoothing back his hair. He straightened his coat and turned around.

"In any case, Miss Elizabeth and her family are still in Lambton." Upon hearing this, Bingley heaved a great sigh of relief and then tried to cover it up by rubbing his stomach in a gesture of exaggerated hunger. He would still have a chance to hear news of Jane! Darcy continued, "I have made arrangements to see them tomorrow morning at the inn where they are staying. After Georgiana arrives, that is. Would you like to join us?"

Georgiana? Why did Darcy wish to introduce Georgiana to Miss Elizabeth and her aunt and uncle? She was so shy that it surely would be torture for her. In any case, Bingley did not wish to talk about Georgiana, in particular why and how he had left her at the mercy of his awful sisters. Never mind that. The important question was: Did he want to visit Miss Elizabeth tomorrow? By Jove, yes, he did!

"Oh, yes, indeed!" he blurted before continuing on with barely suppressed eagerness. "I mean, that sounds capital. It will be delightful to see her again after all this time. I hope her family is well." Her family—especially Jane. Oh, it really was tragic that she had never shared his feelings: the warmth and love and admiration.

"Yes, she said that they are well," Darcy replied with a slight smile. "A number of times."

She said who was what? Lost in his daydream about Jane, Bingley could not remember, but he supposed it did not matter over much.

"I say, old man, I look forward to observing the two of you spar and joust!" he exclaimed with great jocularity. "You and Miss Elizabeth have a great talent for spirited conversation. Perhaps I can learn from you, and it can help me capture the right lady's heart." He still had some doubts about whether that was really what he was looking for in a lady. But he supposed he should jolly Darcy along since it seemed to be what his friend was seeking in a mate.

"Honestly, Bingley, you make it sound as though I have some sort of interest in Miss Elizabeth. Nothing could be further from the truth. I am appalled that you would even joke about such a thing."

Oh dear. Perhaps he had gone too far. Darcy had always made it abundantly clear just exactly what he thought of Miss Elizabeth. So what exactly *was* the man looking for in a lady besides all those things he had listed back in January? Love, connection, sparring, destiny, and so on and so forth, ad nauseam. Oho! At last, he had used a Latin phrase correctly! Or *had* he? Perhaps this was the one that meant "beware of dog." Where was that blasted food?

As if on cue, Mrs. Reynolds suddenly bustled back into the study followed by four footmen straining under the weight of huge platters of food that they set down on the sideboard next to the fire. Bingley saw that all his favourites were indeed included, and he eyed them like a hawk studying a particularly fat and juicy-looking rat. He could barely refrain from hurling himself at the delicious-smelling repast while the servants removed the covers from the dishes. As soon as was decently possible, he began heaping mounds of meat and pies and starchy things onto his plate, his mouth watering. Darcy followed, albeit with less apparent gusto. It seemed he, too, had not yet dined although it was rather later than he usually took his evening meal.

Once Bingley had sat down in his armchair and caused the food on his plate to vanish in a remarkable act of legerdemain, he rested his plate on his knee and relaxed back into his chair to gather energy for a second round of epic indulgence. He hoped that Darcy would join him since Bingley thought he looked a bit poorly, his customary manly glow somewhat dimmed by strain or hunger or whatever it was that had been on his mind lately.

Darcy shook him out of his mid-prandial stupor by saying, "I never did ask, Bingley: What brought you here earlier than expected? What moved you to ride ahead?"

Oh no! Questions about Georgiana! He must deflect!

"Oh, nothing really. Caroline and Louisa were up to their usual tricks: vicious falsehoods, baseless rumours, and gutting criticisms. You know. Caroline in particular was also rattling on about decorations, furniture, lamps, and the like. I must admit that I was paying as little attention as I could while appearing to listen to her."

Suddenly, it struck Bingley that she had been making plans for decorating not their own town house but Pemberley. She had said something about Lady Anne's old rooms…

"Good God, Darcy, you did not give Caroline any encouragement, did you? I know that you were feeling rather low after your visit to your aunt, uh, Lady Clementine?" Had Darcy been so distraught after his cousin refused his proposal that he had done something stupid?

"Catherine. My aunt is Lady Catherine. And no, I did not."

"Perhaps it was something you said by accident? Such as needing a sharp-eyed woman who knew her fabrics and vendors to tend to Pemberley's furnishings? Or perhaps in passing you admired one of her ridiculous hats?" Bingley leaned to his left to cast his eye upon the sideboard, sighing at the neatly arranged platters of steaming meats, pastries, and—oh!—creamed potatoes. He had not noticed those before. And sausages.

"No, of course not, on either count." Darcy shook his head indignantly, and if Bingley were not mistaken—and there was a good chance he was because his stomach had begun emitting an ungentlemanly rumbling—his esteemed friend's nostrils flared. Aha!

Bingley was seized by two warring feelings. Three, if he counted the desperate impulse to spear himself some more parsnips, some cheese, and a large slab of that venison. This third feeling speedily overcame the other two, so he jumped up and positively skipped to the sideboard. As he piled the sausages, parsnips, and other steaming delicacies onto his plate, he mused upon those two remaining feelings.

On the one hand, he was somewhat pleased at the idea of Darcy and his sister as a pair. He had not for a moment seriously considered that Darcy might actually make a match with Caroline. Darcy had always made it clear that he thought Caroline was far beneath him and he could do better. However, there had been an occasional hint about Bingley and Georgiana. Ha—not likely! She was a lovely young woman, a girl really, but far too retiring for Bingley's tastes. No, she could never guide him and nudge him to stay on the mark the way Jane had. He needed that, he realised now. Oh, but Caroline… He knew she and Darcy did not suit even though they did spar, which Darcy had said he liked. But what a delight to consider the possibility that he and Darcy might truly be brothers! To know that forever more they would always be together as a family, as the dearest of chums, and nothing, not even death, could separate them! Well, maybe death. Darcy would certainly end up in heaven, but Bingley was not sure where he himself might go, so selfishly had he left Georgiana to be set upon by his sisters. Yet just imagine all that he could learn from Darcy in the years and months to come and all the ways in which he could grow to be more like Darcy if only they were to become brothers!

On the other hand, Bingley had some grievous concerns about the matter, and on the whole, these concerns outweighed the advantages. Namely, if they were to become brothers, this meant that Bingley would have to spend prodigious amounts of time with Caroline. After all, if they were married, he could hardly see Darcy and visit Darcy's house without seeing Caroline. That would never, never do. He had spent far too many years looking forward to her marriage and her belated and blessed departure from his own household. No, in spite of the certain benefits to having Darcy as his brother, he must end this now, if in fact there was something to end. Bingley unbuttoned his waistcoat and took a deep breath. The loosened clothing and the ability to breathe brought with it greater clarity and a return to his senses.

What was he thinking?! Darcy saw Caroline's true colours; although intelligent and accomplished, she was petty, insecure, and often cruel. She would make him desperately unhappy and drive him to drink. What was it the man had said back in January, on that long-ago night, about suitability trumping love? Yet in April, he would not stop babbling on about love matches. So which was it? Was Darcy still confused, or had he come to his senses as well? The fellow had a book on every subject known to man. And he had read them all! The two theories were diabolically…um, diametrically opposed. He had to make some enquiries on the topic.

But first, some cream cakes. And a duck pasty; surely, he could fit that onto the plate. And more brandy. He caught Darcy's eye and gestured to the bottle on the sideboard. Darcy shook his head and reached for the plum tart on his own plate. He stared at it, and a small smile lit his face before he took a healthy bite. Bingley had not seen Darcy eat with such relish since he had grown eighteen inches and put on two stone during his last year at Eton. He re-joined his friend, easing down into his chair with an eye on the food piled precariously on his plate, and they ate in companionable silence for a moment.

"Bingley, no matter what your sister may think, I shall never marry her." Why was Darcy back on that subject again? Had they not covered it already? Perhaps not; he could not remember what he had *said* and what he had only *thought*. "And I say that with the greatest respect."

"Naturally, naturally." Bingley nodded in relief. He was not offended. He knew his sisters were dreadful. They always had been, and Caroline was an especially unpleasant, shrewish sort of girl.

As the two men ate, the rich, fatty food sank them deeper and deeper into a comfortable, slothful state that only encouraged the exchange of confidences.

Eventually, Bingley could not resist talking about the subject that always floated near the surface of his consciousness: Miss Jane Bennet. He could not speak of her directly, so he chose to speak of her sister and their impending visit. "Darcy, where do Miss Elizabeth and her aunt and uncle stay tonight?"

"In Lambton at the Royal Goat. We shall call there tomorrow as soon as Georgiana arrives." He added softly, "Miss Elizabeth expressed a wish to meet her."

"Did she, now?" How interesting! But why? Perhaps she wished to meet the young lady Caroline had held up as the paragon of accomplished womanhood. Miss Elizabeth was a jolly good girl. He liked a person who could identify admirable traits in another person and then try to emulate them. Rather like himself, truth be told.

Bingley glanced over at Darcy, who seemed to be residing, as he often did, on a different celestial plane, one swarming with men in togas shouting about big ideas and stomping about in impatience with those who would prefer a nice game of whist or cricket. Bingley wondered what the men in Darcy's head were debating this evening. The nature of Justice? The Good? He wished again that he had studied Latin more assiduously so he could understand what it was they were saying. On the other hand, maybe he should just have another pasty instead. He felt he had a bit of room left, and it would please Mrs. R if he ate his fill.

"Bingley, forgive me if you have already answered this question, but where is my sister?"

Oh no. Why did he feel as though he had been caught unawares when in fact he had been dreading just this moment all evening? He had not told Darcy what had become of Georgiana, but then Darcy had not asked so directly prior to now. How should he paint this picture so that all were happily portrayed? "Ah, as you know, I needed to ride ahead and clear my mind. It has been a difficult few months." Eight to be exact. His thoughts were oh-so-lightly touched with bitterness.

"Your sister was enjoying the slower pace of travel and her conversations with her companion. Interesting woman, your Mrs. Annesley. Did you know she has a secret recipe for white soup? She was regaling your sister with tales of her nieces' wedding foibles. They were quite entertained in their own carriage."

Bingley took an enormous bite of roasted hare, chewing it slowly as he awaited Darcy's reply. He was not skilled in hyperbole, and he had stretched his story as far as it would go without breaking, aided only by the meagre intelligence he had gleaned from hearing Georgiana laugh aloud once and ask a question about Mrs. Annesley's family. But Darcy seemed satisfied.

"They are making good time and will arrive in the morning?" Darcy looked a little anxious. Oddly, his anxiety seemed to be more about the projected time of arrival than about Georgiana's well-being. How extraordinary.

"Oh yes." Bingley blew out a great puff of breath in relief, and he would have wiped his brow if he had not thought Darcy would notice. No chastisement. Wonderful.

The edge of Bingley's hunger was just now beginning to dull a bit—but only a bit, mind you—so he rose to fetch himself more sausages and potatoes. He hesitated and then added a bit of apple compote. Jane would have urged him to have some fruit. She had been so particular about the importance of fruit, always gently mentioning something about how it helped keep one from losing one's teeth as the men on sailing ships did. Granted, he was not currently residing on a sailing ship, but he would much rather keep his teeth, so he took Jane's advice and had some apples.

Dropping back down in his leather chair, which now seemed rather slippery and difficult to remain upright in, Bingley sighed a great, happy sigh and tucked in. He speared a huge sausage on his fork and took an enormous bite, as befitted such a great sausage. It was delicious, juicy and meaty, and full of spices he could not name. Fennel? Frankincense? Myrrh? He was not sure.

"Darcy, how did you find Miss Elizabeth's relatives?"

Startled, Darcy sat up and stared at Bingley. "I told you they were touring the gardens. Not far from the pond."

The pond again? He had fallen in, now Bingley was sure of it. He had probably said something in Latin to a horse who knew only Greek.

"Darcy," he articulated slowly, to give Darcy time to take in what he was saying, "I meant: What sort of people were they, the aunt and uncle?"

"Oh." Darcy, who had been worrying his serviette, set it down upon his empty plate and stared at the cloth as it slowly fell out of its twisted, malformed shape. "They were quite interesting. She is from Lambton, as I believe I said before, and he owns some warehouses in Cheapside. Seemed to be quite intelligent about business affairs and is fond of fishing."

Bingley stared, amazed at his friend's unusual loquacity. "Did you entertain them in the house?"

"No, no. We walked a bit through the gardens. Mrs. Gardiner was fatigued, and they declined my offer of refreshments so they could return to the village." Darcy stood and walked over to the window to stare outside at the darkening night sky. "I thought it might be a fine idea to invite the gentleman here for some fishing."

"Capital, Darcy, capital! I look forward to that!" Bingley waved his hands about enthusiastically, mindless of the knife and fork he still held. The giant sausage flew through the air like a porcine projectile recently released from a catapult.

Darcy watched warily, his eyes following the sausage as it flew. "Bingley, please mind the carpet. And the paintings." Well, there was not much he could do about the sausage now, seeing as he did not know where it had landed. As fast as he could, he polished off the remaining meat on his plate. And the apples.

"Oh. My apologies, old man." My God, Darcy sounded like Caroline, lecturing and correcting him. Bingley snickered as he imagined his friend yelling at him in a shrill, high-pitched voice. He stopped when he felt Darcy's perplexed eyes on him. Quickly pulling himself together, Bingley steered to a topic of real interest.

"I never did ask before we left London: Where is the colonel…Archie, I mean, these days? Why has he not accompanied us here? To escape the summer heat in town and all that."

Hands clasped behind his back, Darcy raised his eyebrow and cocked his head at Bingley. "I really cannot say. That is to say, I do not know. I believe he is off on some sort of secret mission or manoeuvre. He must not speak of these things to anyone."

Bingley nodded sympathetically. He hoped that the colonel was safe wherever his hot air balloon was taking him this time. Timbuktu? The Peninsula? The East End? He scraped up the last bit of creamed potato.

"Oh…" Bingley groaned, clapping his plate on the table next to him. He finally felt full. It was even possible that he might have eaten a bit more than he ought. He dropped back into his chair and rubbed his stomach. "I am not sure I can walk to my room. Darcy, you must call for a footman to carry me!"

Darcy laughed. Yes, he laughed! How rare a sight that was these days. It cheered Bingley to his toes to hear the joyful sound. If all it took to make his friend happy was a trip to Pemberley, a good meal, and the prospect of visiting Miss Elizabeth Bennet in the morning, so much the better. That was simple enough. Bingley would see to it that Darcy had cause to laugh more often. Replete, content, and utterly stuffed, he relaxed even deeper into the chair.

Of course, Bingley was also rather keen to see Miss Elizabeth and to hear news of her dear sister Jane. He hoped Jane was well even though she did not love him as he loved her. He hoped she had not already married, started a new life, found happiness with another man. Surely, such a man would not appreciate her goodness, kindness, and gentleness the way that Bingley did. *That* man did not deserve her at all, that man she had married. But wait! He did not know for a fact that she had married anyone. Perhaps there was still hope for him. He must find out. Yes, that was what he would do tomorrow when he met Miss Elizabeth at the Royal Goat. He would use his investigative powers to discover all he could about Miss Jane Bennet.

Perhaps she was still a maid. It had only been above eight months, after all. Perhaps he could find a way to see her again, to discern whether there was any way that such a lovely, devoted, gentle, kind, dear, wonderful, poised woman could ever be persuaded to love a man such as he. He had little to recommend himself, he knew, but he had come to realise that he could not do without her.

Yes, that was what he must do. It would not hurt to ask about Jane. He had nothing to lose except perhaps a bit of pride, and he was not too concerned about all this pride business in any case, not like some people he could name. He was determined. And, once determined, he was content, sure of his path.

Bingley closed his eyes, his hands folded over his belly, and let out a great soughing snore.

Darcy sighed. He rang the bell and contemplatively watched Bingley sleep until a footman entered the room. His friend was no doubt exhausted both from his ride and from the vast amount of food he had just consumed.

"Please have Bingley conveyed to his usual room. There is a sausage under the table and, I believe, a duck pasty wedged between the cushions of his chair. That will be all; I shall see myself to my rooms." He hauled himself to his feet with some difficulty and made his way out of the study and up the stairs to the family rooms, a small smile playing on his lips. He eyed his bed, thinking that it undoubtedly would be a long and sleepless night but not the sort to which he had been accustomed of late, the kind filled with anxiety and hopelessness. This would be different, full of happy anticipation at the thought of seeing Miss Elizabeth Bennet in the morning. He reached for the small leather pouch recently unpacked by his man and laid atop the bureau. He pulled out the delicate handkerchief and hair ribbon and sat down on his bed gazing at them.

Elizabeth.

Part VI: Amare Et Sapere Vix Deo Conceditur

Even a God Finds It Hard to Love and Be Wise at the Same Time

Colours were brighter, food was tastier, the air fresher, and brandy even sweeter and more beckoning to his palate now that he was an engaged man. Bingley could hardly wait to share the joy of his good news with his best friend! Darcy had sent word earlier that he was on his way back from London, where he had gone for reasons he had not made clear. It did not matter. Bingley was bursting with exhilaration.

Finally, the man arrived on Aeschylus, riding up the drive at Netherfield just as the sky was darkening. Bingley bounced out to meet him, hardly waiting till the reins had been handed over to the stable boy before rushing to share the glad tidings of his engagement to Jane.

Darcy was, of course, full of smiles and warm congratulations. Bingley might dare to call the man gregarious in his bear hug and handshake. He knew Darcy was pleased to see him so happily settled, but even he could perceive that the tall, brooding man had yet to forgive himself for prolonging the separation between Bingley and his angel. Naturally, Bingley wished it had not been so long either. After all, what business in London had been so important that Darcy had to run off and leave him at Pemberley, postponing their return to Netherfield for weeks and weeks? But now that was all water under the bridge. After Darcy shook off the dust and washed up a bit, the two men made their way to the study for a drink to celebrate Bingley's joy.

As settled as Bingley was in his own happiness, enhanced by the memory of the sweet kiss Jane had allowed him that afternoon, one glance at Darcy—who was standing tensely at the window of the study, gazing out at the darkness covering Netherfield's park, and twisting that fine signet ring—reminded him that not everyone enjoyed such serenity. Oh, poor Darcy, soon to be surrounded by the happiness of two Bennet sisters and their mother's effusions. Lydia and her new husband were still in the throes of bliss in their newly wedded status, and Mrs. Bennet was in raptures over her handsome son-in-law and his fine red coat. Bingley supposed that his soon-to-be sister's natural ebullience would keep the pair joyful for years, even through the hardships of decamping and moving around the country with the army. At least Wickham had put aside his youthful misbehaviour to earn the hand of Jane's liveliest sister. Had he not overheard Mr. Bennet proclaiming Wickham to be his favourite son-in-law? Odd, then, that the wedding had been such a quiet affair in London.

He glanced at Darcy. His friend, he could see now, had been hesitant when he entered Netherfield. Although Bingley had made it clear that Darcy was welcome to visit at any time and he wished for his friend's quick return, the man's nervous agitation was unsettling. Especially in light of his own great joy and happiness. Earlier today, he had had a difficult time restraining himself from dancing a jig. Even now, he felt as though he might burst into song at the slightest provocation.

But it had been a close thing, really. He recalled—with only a small amount of remaining bitterness—the evening some ten days before when, over brandy and some delicious sandwiches right here in this very room, Darcy had revealed to him the great secret he had withheld from Bingley for so long. It had been quite an evening.

Darcy had begun haltingly. "I greatly regret that I must tell you…what I mean is, regrettably…that is to say, there is something for which I must apologise. Ahem. I must confess that, to my great regret, I kept an important piece of information from you whilst we were in town during the winter."

"Oh, and what was that?" Bingley had asked with some curiosity. Darcy never apologised for anything because he never did anything that warranted it, paragon that he was. What could have brought this on? Was he stewing over something that was not really his fault? And was it significant that he had gulped down two glasses of brandy in rapid succession before beginning his little speech?

With a pained expression on his handsome face, Darcy just managed to squeeze out, "Ahem. Miss Bennet, that is Miss *Jane* Bennet, was in London in January, and she called upon your sisters. They also returned her call. We, I, hid this fact from you."

For once, Bingley was struck dumb. He merely stared at Darcy, unbelieving, the hand holding his brandy glass suspended in mid-air for some time.

Finally, he felt capable of speech. "Why?"

Darcy hung his head. He slowly raised it as he told the tale of the sisters' scheme and his own duplicity in it, well intentioned though it was, to guard Bingley's easily given heart from a beautiful woman of neither great means nor great emotion and her mother with her loudly proclaimed enthusiasm about his income. "Honestly, Bingley. I noticed only Miss Bennet's calm exterior, not grasping that she assumed a mask of indifference to hide great feeling just as I have done so often. I failed you. I am deeply sorry."

Yes, Bingley had been angry. But this was his dear friend, after all. He had been looking out for Bingley's best interests. It was a trespass he could forgive, at least in time.

His sisters were another matter entirely. They had conspired to keep him from his angel! With no concern for anything besides their own social aspirations, they had condemned him to a life of loneliness and misery! He shook with silent fury, imagining how he might confront them about their despicable actions. Why, he would gently chide them for up to a minute—without hurting their delicate sensibilities, of course! Next to their places at breakfast, he would leave sharply worded, unsigned notes, asking that they kindly not commit the same offense again. And he would not bother to disguise his handwriting this time! It was doubtless all Caroline's vile idea. He would creep into her rooms at teatime and punch her favourite flouncy pink pillow over and over again, and then plump it back up so she would not notice he had ever been there! That would show her.

Darcy, though, did not deserve such harsh treatment when his intentions had been kind. Bingley took a deep breath and felt his racing heart calm. Yes, he and Darcy would weather this storm.

He gave his friend a serious look over the top of his glass and said thoughtfully, "Darcy, as long as this is all there is to it, I believe we can put this behind us and think of a happier future."

But Darcy replied, heavily, "Much to my regret, there is still more."

Oh dear.

And then he told Bingley a long and bewildering tale about Miss Elizabeth and his struggles with his feelings for her. Aha! That explained a few things that Bingley had been a confused about, including that mysterious conversation he might have overheard between Darcy and the colonel. Darcy admitted that the woman to whom he had proposed in Kent was not his cousin Anne at all, but Miss Elizabeth. He confessed that Miss Elizabeth had told him then—lo, those many months ago!—that Jane had been in love with Bingley, and his effort to divide them was only one amongst the many reasons Miss Elizabeth had rightly rejected his stupid, ungentlemanly, indefensible proposal of marriage. His interference in Bingley's affairs was officious, reprehensible, and hypocritical. He was filled with remorse for his actions. He begged Bingley's pardon.

Again, Bingley was stunned into silence for some moments. Then, crashing his brandy glass down onto the table, he stood and burst forth with a great bellow of rage. How could Darcy have kept him from Jane for all these months? How could he have withheld the intelligence about Jane's feelings for him? How could he, who had always held himself to the highest standards of truth and honour, have told Bingley such barefaced lies? How could he have kept silent for nearly a year about his own feelings for Miss Elizabeth, not sharing this most important matter with his best friend? Bingley raged on and, if he remembered it correctly, even pounded Darcy's chest with his fists, though Darcy used his longer arms to hold him at bay so he was not able to get in a really good punch.

As it always did, Bingley's anger burnt out quickly. Darcy explained that he felt ashamed at having raised such objections to Jane's family when, as it turned out, he had been quite willing to overlook those things when it came to himself. All of his other behaviour followed from those feelings of shame. Bingley understood *that*, at least. A man as proud as Darcy surely would struggle with such feelings in a way that Bingley never would. Why, he did and said embarrassing things and admitted he had been wrong all the time, and it hardly bothered him at all! But Darcy was not like that. No embarrassing words or noises or stained waistcoats for Darcy!

In any case, was this entire episode worth losing his esteemed friend over? His friend, who had given him so much and been so much to him for so many years? Darcy had apologised quite thoroughly and sincerely, and Bingley saw that he really did regret his actions.

It was a startling realisation that one had to take the good with the bad in a dear old friend like Darcy. He was a good man of excellent breeding, manners, and intellect; he presided over a fine table and a large estate; and he wore a cravat like no other man could. Yet there were aspects to his character that Bingley did not wish to emulate. He had to admit he felt somewhat flattered, maybe even honoured, that Darcy had shared his heartache with him at last, even though it had largely been the cause of Bingley's own sadness.

And now, what did it matter, really? All's well that ends well. Here he was, back at Netherfield and armed with Darcy's assurances that Jane really did reciprocate his feelings; he had proposed to her, and what was more, she had accepted! His beautiful, precious, kind, gentle angel had accepted him!

What further obstacles remained to his total, utter, and complete happiness? None! None at all.

Well, at least two obstacles came to mind. The continued sweet malevolence of Caroline regarding his intention to wed his Angel of Meryton. And the likely tension between Jane's sister and his best friend. Darcy was in love with Miss Elizabeth. Head over heels, heartbroken, desperate, and hopeless. An astounding turn of events that Darcy's heart finally had been touched—and broken—by Bingley's angel's sister! The great man had been humbled by love in a way that neither horse, nor fencing master, nor ill-advised waistcoat had done. Bingley had the edge there, and he could have provided sage advice, but that was of no import now. Indeed, no matter what Darcy had done to keep him from his happiness, he, Charles Horatio Bingley, was now in a position to aid and advise his dearest friend, Fitzwilliam Tiberius Darcy. This opportunity to do such great good for his friend, to affect his life and counsel him on creating his own joy, was indeed rare and precious. He could not fail him even though he remained a bit miffed that Darcy had not turned to him in his own hour—nay, months—of need. Well, he had done so now, more or less. Less, if one were truly honest about it, but again, Bingley would not be petty and look a gift horse or a humbled Darcy in the mouth. Ha! As if he wished to look closely at those impressively straight, pristine, and oh-so-rarely-displayed ivories!

Bingley looked across the room at Darcy, still by the window. He had seen his friend in so many moods this past year, from silent and still with contained fury to politely taciturn, from damply ebullient to painfully contrite. Never, though, had he seen him so openly vulnerable. Darcy was happy for Bingley and Jane and trying hard to hide his melancholy. What a reversal of fortune! *Darcy* needed *his* advice on women, on love. Oh yes. He had to help, to listen and advise. After all, he was an engaged man, assured of the affection of a true angel. Perhaps he could play the go-between, talk to Jane and Elizabeth, and aid Darcy in some reconnaissance? Yes! That was what Archie would do!

Holding firm to this conviction, Bingley said with great assurance, "I am in love with the most perfect woman in the world, she is in love with me, and we are to be wed. And it is all due to you, Darcy, my best friend, the best man in the world. I cannot bear to see you suffer so."

Bingley stood and walked to stand by Darcy's side. He put his arm around Darcy and patted his back. "Come, my friend. You have listened to me talk of my angel and our happily-ever-after. I know you are pleased for us, but it must pain you, alone and broken as you are."

Darcy flinched and began shaking. My God, was the man weeping? No. Darcy would never, ever weep! That was the sort of thing Bingley did occasionally—such as last year when Caroline had slammed the door on his hand in a fit of pique—but never Darcy. He had not even shed a tear after he had been whipped by his father for one of Wickham's misdeeds involving a horse, a kitchen maid, and a jar of gooseberry jam. Darcy had to be in a bad way to be reduced to tears, which prompted Bingley to sputter an apology. "Darcy, I mean no slight, but if you yearn for Miss Elizabeth as I yearned for Jane, then I must intercede and help you. Please, please do not cry."

The taller man pulled away and, to Bingley's surprise, chuckled bitterly, no tears in evidence at all. "I am not weeping. I am laughing at myself and my own stupidity. I, who can read Greek, Latin, Italian, and French, play the violin, and quote Virgil and Shakespeare, and who have been master of my own estate since I was twenty-two, am incompetent in understanding love. I have spent my life running from allurements, entanglements, and entrapments, and it has blinded me to the true worth and honest feelings of a good woman like your Jane."

"Or your Elizabeth."

Darcy paced the room, running his hands through his thick hair and leaving it standing on end. "She is not mine, Bingley." He sighed. "Is it just ladies named Bennet whom I cannot understand, or have I misread the intentions of every lady I have ever encountered at balls, assemblies, and card parties?"

He stalked to the cabinet and poured himself another large serving of brandy. "I have endeavoured to be better at it, but it is difficult to learn how to please a woman worthy of being pleased when I lack the intelligence to judge what is worthy and the words to tell her of her value, her immense and wonderful importance." Brandy bottle in hand, he slid into a chair. "It seems simple enough, but she is...she is not like other ladies. She is so much..." He paused to find the right word. "...better." How odd to see Darcy struggle for a word and finally produce something so prosaic and with so few syllables! Darcy sipped his brandy and stared past his friend at the bookshelves, slightly more populated than they had been in the autumn. Where once there were only *six* volumes (oh, and the one under the seat cushion), there were currently *eighteen* volumes, only five of which were scandalous novels peeping out here and there from between tomes on coin collecting and animal husbandry. Following his friend's gaze, Bingley was proud to see proof of his growth as a gentleman since coming to Netherfield. Just as he was delighted by Darcy's next words, in all their simplicity, about the lady of his dreams: "She is perfect."

Bingley sat in the chair separated from Darcy's by a small table on which the brandy bottle now rested. He stroked his chin and contemplated Darcy's eyes. They were dark and confused, and his brow was furrowed. Tuffy the spaniel used to have that look whenever Caroline had dangled a bit of roast by his nose only to move it away, crying, "Bad dog!" He had not been a bad dog. Only a bit deaf, a little slow, and very sweet. God, Caroline was dreadful. He could only pray she would never have children or come near her nieces and nephews. Oh! He would have to protect their children—his and Jane's babies—from her! Bingley suddenly felt overwhelmed and realised he needed to make a list of all the vital points to remember now that he was to have a wife. He sighed. Jane... Perhaps she could help him write the list and, after that, help him remember where he had put it. Wait...what was Darcy saying?

"Forgive me, Bingley. I am unforgivably morose on this, your happy day." Darcy moved towards Bingley and filled his glass. "A toast to you and your angel."

Bingley took a long drink. Ah, yes. Love did indeed make brandy taste better. Even the French label vintages brought by Darcy. He poured himself just a bit more of the fine stuff.

"Bingley, I am not hopeless. I actually feel there is a chance, albeit small, that Miss Elizabeth has softened somewhat in her feelings towards me. But I have misread and misunderstood her so many times that I feel I must be cautious."

What was this? Darcy was holding onto some shred of hope? "What is it, Darcy, that provides this small ray of sunshine in your heart?" Now that was quite poetic. Love makes us all poets. He should write an ode to Jane! About love, walks in the meadow, puppies, and ginger cake! "There once was a young lady from Meryton…" he mumbled.

"Bingley? Are you attending to the conversation?" Darcy asked. "I do not know how to act. My aunt—"

"Lady Clarabel." Bingley nodded sagely. He sat up a bit straighter, hoping such a posture made him look more attentive.

"—*Catherine*, Lady Catherine, in spite of all her hateful language, did give me reason to hope that Miss Elizabeth might still be willing to look favourably upon my suit. But I do not wish to importune her, to force her once again to reject me if her feelings are still what they were in the spring."

In a small voice, he went on, "And I do not know whether I can bear it if she rejects me again."

Ah, so that was it. This was, perhaps, yet another way in which he and Darcy differed. Bingley was used to being wrong, to being taken down a peg, to looking stupid. But Darcy was not. He was so careful, careful to say just the right thing in the right way using the right words, careful to do precisely the correct thing lest he be misunderstood. That must be difficult indeed. Much more difficult than for a clown like himself even if his smiling visage sometimes hid pain or sadness. Jane would know his feelings. They would sit together and speak not a word while enjoying their breakfast or writing their letters, and she would know whether he was happy or sad, frightened or confident. No, husbands must not be frightened. Cautious, perhaps. Damn, his mind had wandered again. He must reply to Darcy.

"Come, now, Darcy! I think you surely must try! I have seen nothing to indicate she thinks ill of you."

"No, I suppose not. But before I went to London, neither did she offer much in the way of encouragement."

"Perhaps she is unsure of your feelings as well! How could she know that you love her so desperately, old man, when you stand about stupidly instead of speaking to her? You stare at her or look out the windows."

Why *does* Darcy always stare at walls and windows? Archie would never do that. Bingley would never do that either. It was dull to look at landscapes, and he had never understood why anyone looked at stars just to point out his superior knowledge of their names. Icarus? No, Sirius, Romulus, and Remus, the triplets. There, he knew the names of a few stars! Now, clouds—those were another matter. They took on such amusing shapes. They did not *all* look like puffy sheep; indeed, he often saw fish, elephants, and sausages when he gazed at them. What would it feel like to ride a hot air balloon through the clouds? Did you feel them? Could you grab bits and pieces and reshape them? He must ask Archie about that.

The clink of a bottle against his glass pulled Bingley out of the clouds. Darcy had refilled their glasses and was watching his friend with an amused expression.

"What exactly did Lady Corinthian...uh, Catherine say to Miss Elizabeth?" Bingley enquired, abashed at being caught with his attention wandering. He was an engaged man, for God's sake. He must pay attention! And he probably ought to remember something about this particular topic as well because the entire Bennet household had been in an uproar these past few days over the lady's visit. They had all assumed she stopped by on her way to somewhere important to tell the family that the silly parson—Mr. Cuthbert, was it?—and his mousy wife were well. Though perhaps there was more to it because Miss Elizabeth certainly seemed rather tense after the lady left. But when it came right down to it, he had not been paying much attention because he was busy gazing into Jane's eyes, her lovely, lovely eyes...

"The usual rubbish, of course." Darcy shrugged. "She knows no other manner of speaking."

"How on earth did this make you feel more hopeful?"

With utter nonchalance, Darcy replied, "She simply reported she had heard a rumour that, um, Miss Elizabeth and I were betrothed, and Miss Elizabeth had—"

"What?!" Bingley ejaculated. He awkwardly scooted his chair closer to Darcy's, its legs barking loudly on the wooden floor.

"…and that Miss Elizabeth had denied it, but she refused to promise that she never would become engaged to me. Naturally, Aunt Catherine was outraged."

"Naturally! It is obvious, Darcy, Miss Elizabeth loves you." Hurrah! There was really no use in disputing it. Darcy could be quite a dullard about this love business.

"No, I—she may have merely enjoyed contradicting my aunt, who was extraordinarily offensive to her, I believe. Miss Elizabeth does love a good argument."

"Yes, she does," Bingley said fondly. "Not that I would ever dare to argue with her as I already am outmatched by you. And I suspect Miss Elizabeth has a far finer intellect than even you, my friend."

Darcy smiled. "Well, yes. She does spar and joust with great skill. Do you know what else she said, Bingley? She told my aunt that any wife of mine would have so many sources of happiness that she would have no cause to repine. Could that mean what I hope it means?"

"These Bennet sisters are an enigmatic pair, Darcy. But I believe we both own the keys to their hearts." Bingley said that he only *believed* it, but truly, he was *sure* of it. Absolutely convinced.

"Maybe you have the right of it." Darcy sighed. He stretched out in his chair, looking thoughtful in a bleary sort of way.

"Our Miss Bennets are proof that angels walk the earth, Darcy."

The comment provoked a small smile and a sigh from the would-be lover. "Bingley, what is it about your Miss Bennet that first captured your heart?"

"Her smile. Her soft, sweet lips bestowed a most beautiful smile upon me when we danced at the assembly. She wore such a kind-hearted expression whether she looked at me or her sisters or even *my* sisters! And then we walked together in Meryton, and she bent down to greet a child and her little puppy, and my heart was lost to my angel." Bingley smiled softly, his face aglow in the reverie of Cupid's perfectly aimed first arrow.

Darcy nodded. "I saw her eyes, and I was lost."

"I say!" Bingley cried indignantly. "Do you speak of Jane's eyes, man?"

"What? Of course not. Hers are a nice shade of, uh, blue, but it is Elizabeth's dark eyes that captivated and captured me. Their sparkle, their brightness, the deep intelligence and humour within them. I have never seen their like." Darcy rested his chin in his hand. "I hope our children have her eyes," he murmured.

"Oh, I look forward to having a *mob* of children running up and down the stairs, rolling about on the rugs, and splashing in the bath," Bingley exclaimed. He looked at Darcy to expound on his dream. "With Jane's big blue eyes and sweet smiles. Well, not the boys, perhaps. I would prefer they be handsome, not pretty, with strong jaws and broad shoulders and perhaps cleft chins."

His friend bit back whatever he planned to say and instead responded, "That seems possible given that it runs in the family. From whom did Caroline inherit her cleft chin? Did your father have one?"

"Pardon?" gasped Bingley.

"Your sister has a small dimple in her chin. If she has one, then it is likely a family trait, as is mine."

Bingley shook his head. "My sister has no cleft chin. That is a scar from a childhood incident. A battle, if you must know, between an eight-year-old Caroline and our cousin Emily over Emily's china doll. Caroline seized it and would not give it up. My cousin, although smaller, proved the value of having two older brothers. A well-placed punch sent Caroline to the floor, and she struck her chin on the bedpost. She did not bleed much though, considering all the screaming and the resultant damage: a loosened tooth, a ruined frock, some bloodied books."

Darcy chuckled at Bingley's childhood tale. "And their relationship after the brawl?"

"Caroline remains cowed by Emily, who is the quietest of our family and, I believe, quite the most intelligent. If she had not married her true love at seventeen, I would have thought her a good match for you." Bingley laughed. "Oh, imagine it! Ten years on, the two of them could have had another battle, pulling you about by *your* limbs!"

"Ah, drawn and quartered, trussed, and served up," Darcy said drily. "I am happy such a fierce lady found her true love at so young an age. It has taken me much longer."

Bingley sprang up and suddenly felt the effect of his four—or was it six?—glasses of brandy. Would Jane help regulate his intake of spirits or would she disapprove of them altogether and keep them under lock and key? He would not require port when he was rid of Caroline's constant, pestering presence, but he had been imbibing even without her company. It was because of Darcy. His own heartache and Darcy. And Darcy's heartache. Yes, his own heartache, Darcy's heartache, and Darcy, that was it. Well, that was all in the past. His life was tied to Jane now, his heart and his future felicity settled. And it seemed to him that Darcy's might be as well. But first, he had an important request of his friend.

"Before I forget, Darcy, I do need to importune you. I know you and Miss Elizabeth have unfinished business, but I do wish for you to stand up with me on my wedding day, old man."

Darcy looked startled but nodded. "Nothing would please me more. I am overwhelmed that you and your betrothed can forgive my interference and accept me as a friend who wishes only for your greatest happiness." He added wryly, "You are certain you do not wish for Hurst instead?"

Bingley gazed at Darcy, who had one magnificent eyebrow raised in droll amusement. "I enjoy my brother's company, but he has no claims on my friendship beyond his marriage to my sister. Unlike the two of us, he cannot hold his liquor, and you know his lack of skill with a gun or sword.

We likely should keep him away from any and all billiards tables as well. Pointed objects are not his friend."

The two men laughed and sighed, one content and one expectant. Bingley could not wait to get started on this grand new adventure! Why was Darcy dawdling about in this ridiculous manner?

"All right then; that is settled! I am to be married, and now it is your turn. Go to it, man!"

Darcy grimaced and gave no response.

Bingley planted his feet a bit unsteadily and rubbed his hands together. "I have a plan! Just as you watched Jane to ascertain her feelings for me, I shall watch Miss Elizabeth. Tomorrow, with Jane's assistance, I shall do reconnaissance while we all go for a walk. Perhaps, if things look promising for you, Jane and I shall steal away into the shrubbery and leave you two alone."

And the opportunity for kissing lay ahead through such a plan! Bingley needed to ask Darcy once again about exactly where noses should be placed and where hands could safely roam during such kissing forays in the hedges. And were there thorny shrubs they should avoid? How did he judge Mr. Bennet as a protector? Would he stand in the way of their time spent alone in the hedges? On the other hand, should he ask Darcy to be a judge of anyone, considering his recent record?

"Careful, my friend," said Darcy. "You are weaving about like a thirst-crazed bantam cock."

"I am not thirst-crazed! Do not compare me to a cock!"

"Excuse me for speaking imprecisely. You are not thirsty nor are you a bantam cock. You are my best friend, I am your best man, and I am beyond pleased for you."

Darcy put the cork back into the nearly empty bottle of brandy. "You have a day full of happiness awaiting you tomorrow and likely some wedding planning to discuss with Mrs. Bennet. And I have a mission as well. To succeed, I must be at my best, my mind clear and sharp. To bed, we must go."

"Yes, indeed!" exclaimed Bingley. "Tomorrow cannot come too soon."

Darcy stood, and Bingley clapped his tall friend on the back. The two men shuffled a trifle unsteadily out of the room, making their way together towards the happy future each pictured for himself, one already assured of its inevitability, and the other daring to hope it might one day soon be within his reach.

Part VII: Amor Vincit Omnia

Love Conquers All

Tomorrow! Tomorrow he would be a married man! Bingley could not believe his luck. He firmly believed that he was in fact the luckiest man in the world, and he could not wait to begin his new life with his kind, gentle, loving, beautiful angel, Jane. Why were the hands of the clock moving so blasted slowly?!

He was ready to march into the church right now. Unfortunately, Bingley found himself instead in his drawing room at Netherfield with Darcy, Hurst, and Archie, all looking for ways to pass the time until morning when, at last, Bingley and his best friend would stand at the altar together to wed the ladies of their dreams. Already, the colonel, who had proved as free with a bottle of fine French brandy as any man Bingley had ever encountered, had refilled their glasses once, nay twice, while regaling them with stories about his scars and the great gumption shown by his men in fighting Old Boney. But such conversation had dwindled in the face of other preoccupations. The two grooms lacked interest in tales of the battlefield, and despite having eaten a heavy meal not an hour earlier, Hurst was doggedly applying himself to an appreciation of the unexpectedly delightful treats laid out on the sideboard. Bingley turned from watching his gluttonous brother of five years to look upon his brother-to-be. His best friend. His best man. Darcy.

Yes, he could tell that Darcy was nearly as eager as he was, although Darcy was doing pretty well at hiding it. But nothing could disguise the joy in his bright eyes, the glow of his manly cheeks, or the tiny smile that kept threatening to burst forth from the corners of his strong, firm mouth. Also, he kept whistling, seemingly unawares, stopping when he caught himself doing so and then beginning anew once his attention had been diverted elsewhere. Bingley thought the tune was either "Greensleeves" or "Drunken Sailor," but he was not entirely sure which one. He was ecstatic to see his friend in such a state of happiness. Indeed, Bingley himself was positively wriggling in delight and anticipation.

But there were still many hours to wait before the wedding. Bingley doubted that either he or Darcy would sleep much, if at all, that night. The question therefore remained: How could they possibly pass all those annoying, snail-creeping, treacle-trickling, tock-ticking hours until dawn? But if they did not sleep, how would they stay awake and be, ah, prepared for their wedding night with their brides? It was a quandary.

As for how to pass the hours, Darcy's cousin seemed to have some pretty fixed ideas on that subject. Perhaps it was due to his military experience, but as usual, his methods included getting his friends and relations thoroughly sloshed as quickly as possible. Hurst agreed that was an excellent plan as long as copious quantities of meat, cheese, ragouts, potatoes, rich sauces, sausages, cream soup, a fish or two, ices, and cakes were also involved. And some snacks for afterwards, such as nuts and sweetmeats. Bingley enjoyed a good meal but did not wish to further gorge himself this evening for two reasons: first, he feared he might not fit into his snug waistcoat tomorrow, and second, there seemed to be butterflies or some other sort of flying creature resident in his stomach, banging about in a most unfamiliar way. If he understood human anatomy correctly, it was dark in there, so maybe not a butterfly. A small bat, then?

Ha ha! How absurd! There could not really be a bat flying about inside his stomach. Could there? No, not unless one had flown in when he had not been paying attention, dreaming about Jane with his mouth hanging open. It must be nerves. Although Bingley was deliriously happy about the approaching nuptials, he realised that he still had some questions about tomorrow and the days and nights to follow. Quite a few questions actually. A great, massive, tottering, perilously high mountain of them, as a matter of fact. He hardly knew where to begin, really.

First, he had a number of questions about the physics and geometry of the wedding night. What went where, how, for how long, and that sort of thing. With one's own wife, that is. Bingley was a genius with geometry on the billiards table, but he felt somewhat at a loss when it came to geometry in the marital bed. Second, he also had any number of other questions about modern languages and rhetoric; namely, what was one supposed to say, if anything, to one's wife while engaging in, ah…physics and geometry? He really was not sure. He also was not sure that this particular group of men was the right one to answer these questions. The colonel—Archie, that is!— would surely have quite a bit to say on the topic, expert with the ladies that he was. But it seemed to Bingley that, all things considered, his advice might be useful for a single young man sporting at a French house but probably not for a man and his new bride. Darcy would be of no use. Well, he might be, but the pompous old goat would never share whatever knowledge he had gleaned from his own experience or, more likely, his damn books. Darcy's romantic adventures would remain an enigma, an unsolved mystery, and Bingley would never know of them. Once he was a married man, Darcy certainly would never speak about his former conquests. No matter—it would likely involve too many odd languages. Tongues! Bingley giggled.

Jarred back to his senses by the sound, Bingley clapped a hand over his mouth and looked around the room. All was well. No one was looking at him. He stared over at Hurst. Gah! He truly, truly did not wish to hear what Hurst had to say on this subject. The thought of Hurst, Louisa, and conjugal relations together in the same sentence was enough to make the bat in Bingley's stomach begin rocketing around like one of those hot air balloons after it had been hit by a cannonball. Or a mad flock of sharp-beaked crows…

Yet he did need some answers. Would Darcy have packed a relevant book or two? Would they have illustrations? That would rid his mind of such unpleasant visions of his sister and her corpulent husband.

Well, here they all were, stuck in this infernal drawing room with absolutely nothing to do but wait and wait and wait. He might as well see whether he could elicit some information of value from these fellows—poorly equipped or unwilling to act as his instructors though they might be.

Bingley realised that he had been pacing about like a caged tiger and decided he was far more likely to get the serious intelligence he needed if he were sitting down and looking his fellows in the eye. He glanced about and chose the empty leather armchair closest to where Darcy was standing by the window. Bingley coughed to gain his friends' attention.

Darcy turned away from the window to look at him just as Bingley hoped he would. The colonel, seated nearby at the hearth, glanced up from a button he had been worrying on the cuff of his fine woollen jacket. Hurst, on the other hand, could not be deterred from grazing at the groaning sideboard where he was currently engaged in tearing the wings off a goose with his bare hands.

"Well! Jolly fine evening, is it not?" Bingley asked then hesitated. How on earth could he possibly begin this conversation? He cleared his throat, took a sip of brandy, and wiped his mouth with his sleeve. Darcy and the colonel continued to look at him in confusion whilst Hurst finished up his business with the goose and moved on to the pork aspic.

"Is something bothering you, Bingley?" asked Darcy. "You look a bit flushed."

Well, it was now or never. He would never get a better opening than that, so Bingley plunged right in, fixing his gaze at the ceiling. He could not bring himself to look his friends in the eyes after all.

"I am not a child of the farmyard nor the son of a landowner. I know many of my peers learned their lessons about physical love from time spent with cows and horses and sheep and pigs and goats and…"

"Bingley…" Darcy began.

"But I have only lived among my sisters. And dogs," he added, thinking of Tuffy, the ancient, arthritic spaniel and his rather large harem. "I know little of nature's way beyond that. I would like some illumination." Bingley looked up and surveyed his potential instructors. Darcy and the colonel appeared simultaneously confused, aghast, and amused.

"Drawings would be helpful."

At this, Hurst finally turned away from the sideboard to look at his brother sardonically, meat pie in hand.

"Well, it looks so painful and unpleasant with dogs, and there is considerable screeching and barking as a result. But I do not recall any pain, besides the biting, of course, in my own experience. Mademoiselle Angélique, you know," Bingley explained to the other men's horrified ears. What? Was it not customary to speak of the biting? Ah well, in for a penny, in for a pound. "But I have heard a maiden will feel pain, and I fear I shall hurt my dear Jane. She is so delicate.

"I do not wish to harm her," he added quietly. "Darcy? Some advice?"

Darcy, wide-eyed, shrugged. "I have never, not with a maiden." He swallowed and returned his gaze to the windows. "Be gentle and slow and love her, Bingley."

Bingley sighed. "But how? I have perused the *Kama Sutra* but found nothing useful in it." It had reminded him of an ancient Greek athletics contest, full of naked bodies in unlikely positions.

The colonel guffawed. "Then why do you ask for drawings and diagrams from us?"

Bingley cleared his throat and shot him an irritable glance. "I am not stupid. Those are the wild imaginings of the East Indies. Bodies do not bend in such ways. Any fool could see that." Good lord, the colonel could not honestly believe that a well-educated man such as himself would take that mad book seriously.

"Please, Archie. You are the most learned among us, are you not?" Bingley gave the colonel his best ear-to-ear grin, the one that always earned him a pat on the head from his grandpapa.

"Oh yes, Archie, pretty please," whinged Hurst, sputtering with glee and spewing small bits of pastry on his waistcoat.

The colonel groaned. "Darcy, have you no friends with great and worldly experiences to whom you could have introduced this one?" He jerked a thumb in Bingley's direction. "Seriously, man, I think we just need to get him drunk."

"And what of me, Arch?" Darcy sent him one of his fabled dark looks. "You wish to bedevil me with a sore head on my wedding day? I am to be wed tomorrow as well."

"Yes, thus you too must drink more. God knows you have hardly been the life of the party as the most eligible bachelor in town, so let us send you off with a grand salute!" Archie laughed gaily. "You are surely a bit nervous, as well. So many opportunities wasted, nose in your books while my brother and I charmed the ladies. So much you never attempted, so much you never enjoyed…"

Darcy sighed. "Very well. But I—please do talk to him. He is marrying Elizabeth's sister, after all."

Archie sighed and nodded reluctantly before booming, "Bingley, I must have a pen and some paper! All will be revealed in due course!"

Bingley went to the table in the corner where he found some of Caroline's drawing paper and sticks of charcoal. "Will this do?"

"Yes, yes, capital." Archie took the items from Bingley and shuffled through the pages of drawings, most of them studies of a broad-chested, curly-haired dwarf wearing a signet ring on his sausage-like finger. He barked out a laugh but apparently thought better of teasing Darcy, and he pulled out an unmarked page. He began to sketch, his giant moustache twitching as he did so. "There are a number of possibilities, you see…"

Bingley stood behind Archie's chair and peered over his shoulder.

"This here can go here, best achieved from this angle like so… And this one here, number two, as you see, can also be placed here. Not too hard, mind you!"

"Really? You cannot be serious!" Bingley could not help but exclaim.

Archie bent over the paper and expertly sketched a few more curved lines.

"But, but, ladies do not ride astride!" Bingley cried. "They ride side-saddle."

Hurst drew close and stood breathing rather heavily over the colonel's other shoulder. "I say, you have quite the talent with a charcoal. Such a likeness! Such emotion!"

The colonel grinned proudly. "Thank you. I get quite a lot of practise during campaigns when there is not much to do between battles. Lots of idling about, you know. Art and so on." He finished another tableau with a flourish.

"Good lord, Archie! That cannot be right!" Bingley said accusingly. "Surely you are jesting with this one. I see; this whole affair is one great joke to you, is it not?"

The three other men looked at the drawing with careful consideration. Darcy spoke first. "No, I believe that one, at least, is not merely the product of my cousin's fertile imagination. Not terribly likely, perhaps, but entirely possible."

The colonel nodded. "Oh, yes, indeed. I have seen it done."

Bingley blushed, Hurst snickered, and Darcy protested, "Really, Archie. Please spare us the details of your exploits."

Archie laughed at his cousin's prudery. "I notice that in spite of your protests, all three of you have rather flushed cheeks and dilated pupils. Shall I proceed?"

"You know I do not care terribly for this kind of thing," said Darcy, inching a bit closer and looking at the sketches out of the corner of his eye.

Taking his lead, Bingley nodded and added, "No, nor do I. Please, feel free to stop any time." He too peered more closely at the paper.

"Oh, by all means, do go on," said Hurst jovially. "The beauty of the human form and all that." He rubbed his hands together expectantly and leaned in.

For nearly ten long minutes after the colonel's diagrams had been thoroughly discussed and then burnt in the fireplace, not a word had passed the lips of any of the four men arrayed about the room, but the atmosphere was anything but sedate. The tapping of one man's foot, the clinking of the brandy bottle against an oft-emptied glass, the jingling of coins in a pocket, and the pacing of boots across the oak floor created a rhythm silently observed by a patient hound curled up against the bookcase.

Finally, Bingley could not stand the silence any longer. He felt compelled to change the subject to anything, *anything* other than the uncomfortable, rather improper things of which they had just spoken and the images they had seen. Anything at all. He cleared his throat.

"Archie," he said in a strangled voice. "I have been wondering about clouds."

The colonel paused in his pacing and stared at Bingley. After a quick glance at a bemused Darcy, his hand now stilled and his pence at rest, he turned back to his inquisitor. "Yes, Bingley? Clouds?"

"Yes, well, I have been wondering about the shapes."

The colonel slowly sank down on the ottoman in front of Bingley. "The shapes?

"Yes!" Bingley leaned forward and began gesturing, curving his hands into spirals and swooping them up and down. "Yes, the clouds. Have you ever leaned out of your hot air balloon and touched them and tried to mould them? Like a god in the heavens?"

The colonel, his mouth agape, turned around and met his cousin's eyes. Darcy was of no help, too busy biting back a laugh. "Bingley," the colonel sputtered, "I do not have knowledge of these subjects. I have never touched a cloud. I have never had the opportunity to ride in a hot air balloon." He stared at the younger man, bewilderment spread across his features.

Across the room, Hurst snorted. "Methinks my brother has tippled a little too much."

Bingley narrowed his eyes in perplexity, and suddenly, it dawned on him. Of course! He nodded sagely at his regimental friend. "Ah. Secret missions, eh? Nothing you can tell us? Dash it all, it seems to me to be a romantic way to see the world. You are a fortunate man, my friend. And likely far safer from Boney's bullets. One cannot shoot upwards to reach such a fine apparatus, especially through those puffy wet masses."

"Yes, it is a shame my learned cousin can share so much about the shape and feel of a woman, but cannot speak of the feel and contour of a puffy wet mass," Darcy said slowly. "I thought you might know something of that as well." He stared dolefully at Archie, whose glare suddenly softened into an amused smirk.

"Ah yes. There is something else, Bingley, that I must share with you. Excuse me a moment." The colonel slipped out the door, returning a short time later stroking his chin and looking excessively serious.

"Bingley, did your father or your uncle—the one who took you to that French house that time?—ever speak to you of cautionary practices? Of the dangers of carnal knowledge with an unknown lady?"

Bingley shook his head from side to side, and his eyes widened. "No," he whispered.

All eyes were on the colonel as he began his woeful tale of soldiers stricken by a love bug that shrivelled their man parts, created oozing pustules, and crippled their limbs. He turned away from his gaping audience of Hurst and Bingley and winked at Darcy. "And this, Bingley," he roared, pantomiming a reach into his small-clothes while turning suddenly and thrusting his hands towards the frightened man, "is what can happen to a man who looks for love in all the wrong places!"

Bingley screeched. Hurst gasped. Darcy slid down the wall and onto the floor, laughing uncontrollably. The colonel dropped a crumbled cherry tart onto a plate and wiped his hands. He sat down in dramatic fashion and awaited the room's return to sanity.

Hurst was first. "Zooks, that was a fine-looking tart, Arch! It did not touch anything, did it?" He reached for the lovely little pastry, though he waited for the colonel's negative reply, hand poised over the plate, before picking it up and taking a bite.

Darcy only laughed harder. As Bingley recovered himself, his heart pounding and his mind still reeling, he focused on Darcy's laughter. Was the man hysterical? With fright? And why did he not laugh like that more often? He had an attractive, musical laugh, in the baritone range, which truly was quite beguiling. He would make a note to ask Miss Elizabeth whether she liked Darcy's laugh. He wondered what she thought of his cleft chin as well. She had likely touched it, lucky girl. Jane would like him to have a cleft, he was sure of it. Even one created through violent battle like Caroline's. Perhaps he should ask her.

Wait, that reminded him! Talking! If they were to be touching, they had to be talking. Bingley recalled that bit of advice from an uncle or some such relative. Oh! It was his bearded aunt, he now remembered, telling him to sit up straight, hold her hand, and talk. Ah, Auntie Florabella. How Caroline hated her. How she hated Caroline. Bingley had enjoyed his aunt's visits, always the favourite little flaxen-haired lad, fearless and admiring of her chin whiskers. *When you sit close and hold hands, Charlie,* she had said, *you must always have some conversation.* Surely, this must also hold true with other sorts of intimate contact. But what, precisely, must one say in such a circumstance? Certainly, one must speak neither of one's arthritis and bunions nor of one's digestive shortcomings, these having been his two major topics of discussion with Auntie. That did not seem right at all. What then? He needed to know. It was all so complicated. There were so many things he had to remember at the same time about how to please Jane: talking, kissing, touching… How could he possibly remember to do all these things at once? He worried that he might get carried away with one and forget the other two.

It had not been so complicated that one other time with Mademoiselle Angélique. He shuddered, recalling how confused he had been about using his hands. One here? The other there? Or there? He had decided that the safest and speediest route to getting the event to its climax was to keep his hands to himself and simply enjoy the great pleasures she wrought with her hands and her tongue and her teeth. Well, perhaps not her teeth. They had been so sharp, nibbling at his fleshy bits. He had not been able to think for the entire quarter hour he had been with her, but he had recalled far, far too much of it afterward. Especially the teeth, so small, white, and spiteful.

Bingley stood up, albeit unsteadily, and walked an uneven path to the sideboard. He poured a tall glass of brandy, drank half of it in one great gulp, and returned to his seat. Smacking his lips, he stared straight at Darcy. "Thank your cousin for his exhibition, Darcy. But now, I must ask you, the most learned among us, about, um, *dialogue*."

Darcy's reddened face slowly returned to a normal colour and he took on a perplexed expression. "The Platonic dialogues? You ask me to speak of Sparta and the Greeks?" Bingley shook his head no. "Do you refer perhaps instead to the theatre? Do you wish me to recite dialogue from the Bard?"

"No, no!" Bingley cried. "You know books, Darcy! You have read them all! You know the epic poems and tales, *Le Morte d'Arthur, Tristan and Isolde, Hansel and Gretel,* the great courtly romances, all by heart! You must tell me the words, the poetry, shared by a man and his wife when they are engaged in…ahem…literary discourse." He sat up straighter and took a long drink. "I demand my share of your knowledge."

Darcy stared at him, all astonishment. "You ask this of *me*? A man so inept in the art of wooing and courting that he could not even properly propose in a civil manner the first time? A man who insulted and hurt and angered the woman he loved?"

The chomping noises that had kept them company for some minutes ceased as Hurst cried out, "What was that, now?"

"He truly is no linguist, Bingley," averred the colonel. "Though he pens a fine letter, I must say. All the family, and I include the future Mrs. Darcy in that group, enjoy his descriptive letters." Darcy skewered him with a fierce glower. "And fine penmanship. He must mend his pens quite often." He collapsed into a chair, chuckling merrily.

Bingley shook his head in confusion. "Yet you wooed her, Darcy! You won the heart of one of the most witty and intelligent ladies in the land. And now you two spar and laugh, your tongues twisting words into *bon mots,* which leads to some impassioned kissing if I do say so myself."

Darcy's eyes narrowed. "Oh, I think you must *not* say, my friend. A gentleman never does."

Bingley flushed. He knew he should not have watched them that afternoon in the garden, but he had been hoping for some pointers. He had seen glimpses of kisses and caresses, and the heated looks exchanged between the two lovers, but their words had been indecipherable. The birds had been too loud, the rustle of hands on fabric too distracting, and the tension in his arm too painful from holding down the branches so he could more clearly view the romantic scene. But things had been said, words and coos exchanged. He had heard Darcy moan, for goodness' sake! At first, he thought Miss Elizabeth had pulled the poor man's hair, and he was crying out in pain, but in fact, shortly thereafter, it had become clear that Darcy had liked whatever it was she was doing to his neck. It was not clear whether any biting had been involved; both parties had nice white teeth, but Bingley had not seen them bared.

So was that the secret? Cooing and sweet gentle murmurings? Teasing and tickling? He and Jane had kissed. Many times, in fact, over these past few weeks. But he had never dared to kiss her as, ah, enthusiastically as he had seen Darcy kiss Miss Elizabeth. There had been neither moaning nor mewling between him and Jane. But their kisses still filled him with such a feeling of rightness, of warmth, of full and complete happiness. So tomorrow night, yes, he would give it a try, the cooing and murmuring and teasing and so forth.

Oh, this was all so daunting! He needed more brandy. Especially with Darcy still glaring at him.

Despite the great man's somewhat justified irritation with him, Bingley was overjoyed that Darcy would, on the morrow, become his brother. And so much the better that it was not by means of Darcy's marrying Caroline! My God, how could that thought ever have crossed his mind? Blasted brandy. Sweet nectar with the most damnable consequences.

Bingley need never fear that one day he would lose his friend's wise counsel. He would always have someone to turn to when he had questions about poultry, drainage, financial instruments, or love. Well, perhaps not questions about love. Darcy was right when he said he had some deficiencies in regard to speaking about love. And after all they had been through in the past year, and after this evening's conversation, Bingley thought that perhaps he might be better off relying on his own judgment in matters of the heart, more broadly speaking. Take the entire sparring and jousting disaster, for instance. Or Darcy's ridiculous, ever-changing views on the importance of social standing in choosing a wife. Never! It was love—true love—that mattered! Ah, Jane, his angel.

Yes, Bingley might follow Darcy's advice about the cut of a waistcoat, proper fencing etiquette, or other practical matters, but he was through with such queries when it came to love. Bingley was his own man now. A man about to become a husband! And one day a father, he hoped, truly the head of his own family and not just a hapless sheepdog nipping at the heels of his two vile sisters, two ewes running wild and trampling the garden. Baa, baa. He wished instead to become a truly accomplished shepherd for his family with his lovely shepherdess by his side. He could imagine her blue eyes shining in the sunlight, tall crook in hand, his own beautiful Bo Peep. With Jane beside him, there would never be any lost little lambs. Together they would fend off lamb-eating wolves. And his sisters.

Was the colonel a magician? Bingley could swear he had already drained the last drop from his glass, the last drop he planned to swallow. All the better to keep his head for tomorrow. So why was his glass always full? Or had he forgotten to drink the last serving? Hmm.

"I do hope that Caroline and Louisa will keep their spite and vitriol to themselves tomorrow, old man, but I fear the worst," Bingley said to Darcy with regret. "They are just dreadful. They always have been."

Darcy looked sharply at Hurst as though concerned that he might take offense at Bingley's words. Hurst waved him off, muttering, "No, no, he is quite right. Quite so. But Louisa is my sweet pea, nevertheless." Hurst sighed and closed his eyes, leaned back in his chair, and released an enormous belch. He opened one eye and glanced about at his audience. "You see, Louisa may indeed have a sharp tongue, but that is only when her sister is in the room."

Hearing Bingley scoff, Hurst sat up. "Bingley, think on this. Has Louisa ever been deliberately cruel to you, or has she simply withdrawn from a confrontation with her sister? My wife is a shy girl who has been ever overshadowed by her quick-witted, ill-tempered sister and her brother, the fair-haired only son."

"You have determined this over the past few years?" Bingley asked, stunned both by such a perceptive disclosure and by his sedentary brother's hitherto hidden skills of observation.

"Of course not, you dolt; she told me. Tells me every chance she gets, and I kiss her to make it all better." Hurst smiled like the cat who ate the canary. "It is the precursor to many an enjoyable evening, I must tell you."

"No!" cried two voices. "Do not tell us!"

The shrieking grooms busied themselves with various matters involving brandy and observations about the stars peeking through the clouds.

Archie chuckled. "Boys, you two are on the threshold of marital paradise. Both of you are men who will be true and constant to your wives. May you soon find your own harbingers of evenings full of delight. I raise a toast to years of connubial bliss. For you all," he added, nodding in Hurst's direction.

Hurst rose and adjusted his coat. "As the room's sole married man, I shall beg pardon and go listen to my dear wife's complaints. I am sure"—he glanced at Darcy—"that she has had a most trying evening with her sister. I fear her gown may be soaked through with crocodile tears." He winked at Bingley and smiled in what Bingley found a most salacious manner. Salacious meant hungry, did it not? But it was not possible for Hurst still to be hungry, was it?

Darcy looked aghast as his cousin, in answer to Hurst's words, began to recite iambic pentameter, his great moustache quivering with emotion.

"O devil, devil!
"If that the earth could teem with woman's tears,
"Each drop she falls would prove a crocodile.
"Out of my sight!"

"For God's sake, Archie!" snapped Darcy. "*Othello?* Shut it."

Bingley looked anxiously at Hurst. He was not planning to kill Louisa, was he? That seemed unlikely given his earlier comment about, ah, enjoyable evenings with her. But then, who would have guessed that Othello would kill Desdemona? Actually, anyone with half a brain in his head could have seen that one coming from Act I. Well, it had been an utter surprise to him, though admittedly his attention had been diverted by the lovely young lady in the adjacent box. In any case, he would much rather think about happier occasions, such as weddings for example. Quickly, which of the other Shakespeare plays had a wedding in it? Oh! *Romeo and Juliet!* Wait, no, that was hardly much of an improvement over *Othello.*

Um, the one with the shrew for a wife? Lots of yelling until they kissed. He gasped. That seemed familiar, a bit like Darcy and Miss Elizabeth! Except, of course, that Darcy did not want his future wife to be tamed. No, not at all, if he was to be believed about all that sparring and jousting. Not to mention the rustling in the shrubbery! Miss Elizabeth had free rein over the man's neck, it seemed! His cravat was perpetually askew these days. He wondered whether Mr. or Mrs. Bennet had noticed their daughters' swollen lips and ruffled hair whenever they returned from a stroll in the gardens with their betrotheds. Jane had especially soft, silken hair. He would never say a word about it to Darcy, but he believed Jane's blonde tresses were superior to the oft-tangled, dark waves sported by Miss Elizabeth. Often, there were bits of leaves and stalks of grass stuck in her thick locks. He could not imagine what Caroline would say if she chanced to observe her. Well, actually, he supposed he could imagine it well enough.

There was much to admire about Miss Elizabeth as she too was an angel in her own way, but no one could compare to his Jane. Bingley realised he must be careful never to voice such feelings aloud. It would surely lead to a duel with his best friend. How awful that would be. Darcy had Archie. Who would be Bingley's second? Hurst? No, by God, the only person he ever wanted as his second was Darcy, and that would be impossible if the two of them were shooting at one another. That would never do.

The slamming of the door upon Hurst's exit brought Bingley's attention back to the room. He looked over at his friend and noticed that Darcy appeared upset about something. Good lord, had he read Bingley's mind? He must stop thinking these terrible thoughts, or there really would be a duel one day. He must change the subject right away, or before he knew it, he would be facing Darcy with pistols at dawn! And on their wedding day, no less! And Jane would cry; though not as a bride, yet neither as a widow. Crocodile tears would flood the streets of Meryton, creating little biting lizards that would swarm the town! Perhaps he was still a bit unclear on the meaning of the phrase "crocodile tears." He never could understand Shakespeare. Except sometimes the comedies. Was not the one where the shrewish one was tamed by a strong man a comedy? He glanced once more at Darcy and found the man staring thunderously at his cousin.

"Honestly, Archie. *Othello* on the eve of a wedding?" Darcy huffed.

"Sorry, old man." Archie smirked.

Oh, yes—quickly! Change the subject!

"Darcy! Another brandy? Another toast to our brotherhood?"

"I think not. I believe I had best go to my chambers. I have a poem I would like to read. Something a bit more in the spirit of the day." Darcy looked pointedly at the colonel.

Archie rolled his eyes. "Sometimes I wonder what the lively Miss Elizabeth sees in my staid cousin. Though I am glad she recognises his finer points and hones his duller bits." He burst out in unrestrained laughter. Perhaps it was the jerky motions of his moustache or the boisterous knee slapping, but soon both Darcy and Bingley were chuckling along.

"I have no dull bits, Cousin. I am, however, more keenly sharpened and fully witted when I am with her." Darcy lapsed into a dreamy state signalled by the toothy grin Bingley had grown to admire.

Bingley gazed fondly at his friend. Darcy truly was the best of men. Bingley's best friend. No, he was not perfect as Bingley had once thought. He had a brilliant mind. He was the best master, the best brother, the most loyal companion, the most accomplished sportsman, and, furthermore, the owner of the broadest shoulders and the best seat Bingley had ever seen. Not to mention his handsome face and magnificent cleft chin. But he was also a proud man, perhaps a bit too proud even if it was mostly justified. Miss Elizabeth seemed to have worked wonders in curbing that tendency though. And he did seem to have some peculiar ideas both about love and about one's position in society, though Miss Elizabeth did seem to be having a most salutary effect there as well. My goodness, she was just what Darcy needed to become the paragon Bingley had thought he was for all those years! How splendid.

Bingley had to admit that he had secretly been a bit jealous of Miss Elizabeth for a while there. But that was all in the past now that he had his Jane to love. What would be the point in feeling jealous about losing Darcy's attention when Bingley had everything he had ever wanted in the world in his wonderful, kind, gentle, loving, and, yes, beautiful, Jane? She never had twigs in her hair, her slippers were always clean, her hands soft, and she smelt of lovely things like rosewater and lilacs. Even in November!

Bingley looked over at Darcy and noticed that he was still gazing off into space with a besotted smile on his face. He wondered whether that was how *he* often appeared to others. Probably not. He hid his little flights of fancy rather well.

Presently, Archie stopped laughing at his two friends long enough to stand and walk to his cousin, whom he slapped on the shoulder. "Well, old man. You are obviously of no further use to me this evening. Off with you! Go off to your blasted musings and prepare in solitude to enter the bonds of matrimony!"

Darcy shook himself out of his dreamy state long enough to scowl. "Shut it, Archie. They are hardly bonds! Unless they are the gentle bonds of felicity, the joyous chains of love."

Archie smirked. "Certainly, if you find that sort of thing pleasing. Somehow I had thought your interests ran in a different direction."

"You are incorrigible! I cannot stand this another moment." Darcy stood, looked about the room, and nodded as if coming to a decision. He walked over to Bingley and grasped his hand briefly before pulling him into a quick hug. Bingley pounded his back in return, too moved to speak.

"Bingley, we are to be brothers, and nothing could make me happier than to forge that connection." Darcy pulled back and smiled. "Nothing, of course, besides marrying Elizabeth. We shall be the happiest of men, the best of brothers, and the worthiest of husbands."

Bingley and Archie stood wordlessly as Darcy's voice dropped to a whisper. "We have lost our parents, so we shall create new families. Together. My parents and yours would be pleased with our brides."

Darcy gave the two men an intense look. "I thank you both for your friendship, your advice, and your companionship on these many evenings." Too overcome with feeling to speak, Bingley nodded vigorously at his friend.

Darcy turned and walked towards the doorway. "I hope you have found fair recompense in drinking and spilling my fine brandy. I consider it all a fine trade." He wheeled around, grinning at the guffaws from the two men.

"And now, I am off to think on a pair of fine eyes and get some sleep. I wish to have the sense and keen wit to appreciate my bride tomorrow."

"And not stumble over your vows," cried Archie to Darcy's retreating back. He stroked his moustache and turned a sharp eye on Bingley. "My cousin was clearly a lost cause. You, however, still show rather a lot of potential in the area of drinking deeply and with great feeling." He raised the glass of brandy in salute and sauntered towards Bingley.

Bingley recoiled. "No, no indeed, I thank you, no, Archie! I believe I have had enough brandy for this evening, and indeed, I do not believe I shall ever touch brandy again after tonight." Now he understood better how a deer felt when looking up the barrel of a gun.

"One last drink as a single man!" Archie said with a wolfish smile. He shoved a glass into Bingley's hand and put an arm around his shoulders. "Bingley, you seem in need of wise counsel. I should like to share a bit of advice with you."

What happened next was never clear to Bingley. In years to come, the events of that night and others spent with Darcy and Archie as bachelors enjoying libations ran together in his mind, all reduced to fleeting images of genies on magic carpets, hot air balloons, puffy sheep-like clouds, bats careering around in his abdomen, mortally wounded billiards tables, and, of course, brandy. Lots of brandy. There were also new, inexplicable images of himself sword fighting in a mirror and an extremely menacing rabbit with blood dripping from its fangs. But he was never sure whether those things had truly happened. Bingley was certain only that he would never again eat cherry tarts or drink more than one glass of brandy. It was all quite a haze, like Latin class or mathematics. In fact, the next moment in time that Bingley could clearly remember after Archie handed him that last glass of spirits was the instant Darcy patted his shoulder, assured him the Netherfield servants had cleaned up the debris and removed the stains, and nodded at him to direct his attention to their brides approaching them from down the aisle.

Oh. Oh! The soon-to-be-former Bennet sisters were indeed the Angels of Meryton! God help him and Darcy to be the men that these angels deserved. Mortal men married to angels. Jane would be the making of him. He gulped, took a deep breath, and glanced at Darcy. His friend's eyes glowed fiercely at his bride—they were even suspiciously bright and shiny—but there was not so much as a quiver in his cleft chin.

How very interesting. How very Darcy.

~The End~

Acknowledgment

DEEPEST THANKS TO OUR EDITOR GAIL WARNER FOR HER MASTERY OF ALL things Regency and her wonderful sense of humor, and to Ellen Pickels for her awe-inspiring knowledge of proper comma placement and, with Janet Taylor's invaluable assistance, a wonderful cover.

About the Authors

JUSTINE RIVARD IS A VERY SERIOUS COLLEGE professor who has no time for frivolity or poppycock of any kind. She strenuously objects to the silliness found in this story and urges you to put the book down at once before it gives you ideas. You are invited instead to join her in the study for a lecture about her extensive collection of whimsical eighteenth-century animal husbandry manuals.

J. L. ASHTON, ON THE OTHER HAND, IS A VERY unserious writer of Jane Austen variations you might have read and a collector of recipes she will never attempt. She encourages a general lack of decorum and has a great appreciation for cleft chins, vulnerably brooding men, and Instagram accounts featuring animals. Especially cats. Also foxes.